Sophy

The Journal of Inspired Writing

Number One

A journal of inspired writing, as expressed by the most out-standing examples of prose and poetic writing in English and other languages, such as American. The content of each issue of **Sophy** is selected to inspire hours of enjoyable reading—and to ignite even more hours of contemplative thinking about life and its meaning.

Sophy is published quarterly by Kudzu House. Address all inquires to: P.O. Box 297, Marble Hill, GA 30148. Telephone: (770) 664-4886.

Carl Japikse, Publisher.
Leslie Ishige, President.
Rose M. Japikse, Production Manager.

Published in the United States of America.

Subscriptions to **Sophy** may be purchased for $32 a year. Please see page 160 for complete details.

Sophy prints only pieces that have already been issued in some other format. We do not accept manuscripts for consideration. All unsolicited manuscripts will be returned unopened to the submitter, at his or her expense.

ISBN 0-89804-600-9
ISSN 1522-6263

We welcome letters from subscribers and readers concerning the nature of the magazine, including suggestions for the content of future issues.

Inside

Sophy — Number One

ON THE FRONT COVER
"The Poet and His Inspiration"
by Nicolas Pouisson

Sophy

Is it a magazine? Is it a book? We're not sure. It may be a book that started out as a magazine, only to grow in stature. It is certainly a periodical, but timeless in content and readability.

And what does the title mean?   Is it the publisher's favorite private label of beer?   Or is it a tribute to Bette Midler's personal hero?

Neither. "Sophy" is a Greek name meaning "wisdom." You've seen it dozens of times before, in old familiar words like "philosophy" and other, less familiar words such as "anthroposophy." It means the same in each instance: wisdom.

Sophy comes into this world for one reason: there is a need for her. It is not just that there is a need for wisdom, which almost goes without stating; but there is also a need for renewed interest in the rich legacy of English writing. Thousands of brilliant, insightful stories and novels have been published in the past few centuries, yet only a handful are ever read and enjoyed—even by well educated people, unless they happen to go to graduate school in English. This is a shame—but one that can be corrected, we hope. By Sophy.

Sophy is designed to be a collection of great stories, essays, and poems by outstanding English authors that can be picked up at the airport and read as entertainment while you are jetting from Albuquerque to Atlanta. Or enjoyed on a quiet evening by the fire, with a glass of sherry and no one but yourself—or, even better, read out loud to a charming companion. Our goal is to restore the art of reading.

Goethe wrote: "A person should hear a little music, read a little poetry, and see a fine picture every day, in order that worldly cares may not obliterate the sense of the beautiful which God has implanted in the human soul." *Sophy* has been conceived to help you do so.

THE SECRET SIN OF SEPTIMUS BROPE

A Story by Saki (H.H. Munro)

"**W**HO and what is Mr. Brope?" demanded the aunt of Clovis suddenly.

Mrs. Riversedge, who had been snipping off the heads of defunct roses, and thinking of nothing in particular, sprang hurriedly to mental attention. She was one of those old-fashioned hostesses who consider that one ought to know something about one's guests, and that the something ought to be to their credit.

"I believe he comes from Leighton Buzzard," she observed by way of preliminary explanation.

"In these days of rapid and convenient travel," said Clovis who was dispersing a colony of green-fly with visitations of cigarette smoke, "to come from Leighton Buzzard does not necessarily denote any great strength of character. It might only mean mere restlessness. Now if he had left it under a cloud, or as a protest against the incurable and heartless frivolity of its inhabitants, that would tell us something about the man and his mission in life."

"What does he do?" pursued Mrs. Troyle magisterially.

"He edits the *Cathedral Monthly,*" said her hostess, "and he's enormously learned about memorial brasses and transepts and the influence of Byzantine worship on modern liturgy, and all those sort of things. Perhaps he is just a little bit heavy and immersed in one range of subjects, but

Saki, the pen name of H.H. Munro, pays homage to the cup bearer in The Rubaiyat of Omar Khayyam. *Saki wrote some of the finest satires of the early 1900's.*

it takes all sorts to make a good house-party, you know. You don't find him *too* dull, do you?"

"Dulness I could overlook," said the aunt of Clovis: "what I cannot forgive is his making love to my maid."

"My dear Mrs. Troyle," gasped the hostess, "what an extraordinary idea! I assure you Mr. Brope would not dream of doing such a thing."

"His dreams are a matter of indifference to me; for all I care his slumbers may be one long indiscretion of unsuitable erotic advances, in which the entire servants' hall may be involved. But in his waking hours he shall not make love to my maid. It's no use arguing about it; I'm firm on the point."

"But you must be mistaken," persisted Mrs. Riversedge; "Mr. Brope would be the last person to do such a thing."

"He is the first person to do such a thing, as far as my information goes, and if I have any voice in the matter he certainly shall be the last. Of course, I am not referring to respectably intentioned lovers."

"I simply cannot think that a man who writes so charmingly and informingly about transepts and Byzantine influences would behave in such an unprincipled manner," said Mrs. Riversedge; "what evidence have you that he's doing anything of the sort? I don't want to doubt your word, of course, but we mustn't be too ready to condemn him unheard, must we?"

"Whether we condemn him or not, he has certainly not been unheard. He has the room next to my dressing-room, and on two occasions, when I dare say he thought I was absent, I have plainly heard him announcing through the wall, 'I love you, Florrie.' Those partition walls upstairs are very thin; one can almost hear a watch ticking in the next room."

"Is your maid called Florence?"

"Her name is Florinda."

"What an extraordinary name to give a maid!"

"I did not give it to her; she arrived in my service already christened."

"What I mean is," said Mrs. Riversedge, "that when I get maids with unsuitable names I call them Jane; they soon get used to it."

"An excellent plan," said the aunt of Clovis coldly; "unfortunately I have got used to being called Jane myself. It happens to be my name."

She cut short Mrs. Riversedge's flood of apologies by abruptly remarking:

"The question is not whether I'm to call my maid Florinda, but whether Mr. Brope is to be permitted to call her Florrie. I am strongly of opinion that he shall not."

"He may have been repeating the words of some song," said Mrs. Riversedge hopefully; "there are lots of those sorts of silly refrains with girls' names," she continued, turning to Clovis as a possible authority on the subject. " 'You mustn't call me Mary—' "

"I shouldn't think of doing so," Clovis assured her; "in the first place, I've always understood that your name was Henrietta; and then I hardly know you well enough to take such a liberty."

"I mean there's a *song* with that refrain," hurriedly explained Mrs. Riversedge, "and there's 'Rhoda, Rhoda kept a pagoda,' and 'Maisie is a daisy,' and heaps of others. Certainly it doesn't sound like Mr. Brope to be singing such songs, but I think we ought to give him the benefit of the doubt."

"I had already done so," said Mrs. Troyle, "until further evidence came my way."

She shut her lips with the resolute finality of one who enjoys the blessed certainty of being implored to open them again.

"Further evidence!" exclaimed her hostess; "do tell me!"

"As I was coming upstairs after breakfast Mr. Brope was just passing my room. In the most natural way in the world a piece of paper dropped out of a packet that he held in his hand and fluttered to the ground just at my door. I was going to call out to him, 'You've dropped something,' and then for some reason I held back and didn't show myself till he was safely in his room. You see it occurred to me that I was very seldom in my room just at that hour, and that Florinda was almost always there tidying up things about that time. So I picked up that innocent-looking piece of paper."

Mrs. Troyle paused again, with the self-applauding air of one who has detected an asp lurking in an apple-charlotte.

Mrs. Riversedge snipped vigorously at the nearest rose bush, incidentally decapitating a Viscountess Folkestone that was just coming into bloom.

"What was on the paper?" she asked.

"Just the words in pencil, 'I love you, Florrie,' and then underneath, crossed out with a faint line, but perfectly plain to read, 'Meet me in the garden by the yew.' "

"There is a yew tree at the bottom of the garden," admitted Mrs. Riversedge.

"At any rate he appears to be truthful," commented Clovis.

"To think that a scandal of this sort should be going on under my roof!" said Mrs. Riversedge indignantly.

"I wonder why it is that scandal seems so much worse under a roof," observed Clovis; "I've always regarded it as a proof of the superior delicacy of the cat tribe that it conducts most of its scandals above the slates."

"Now I come to think of it," resumed Mrs. Riversedge, "there are things about Mr. Brope that I've never been able to account for. His income, for instance: he only gets two hundred a year as editor of the *Cathedral Monthly*, and I know that his people are quite poor, and he hasn't any private means. Yet he manages to afford a flat somewhere in

Westminster, and he goes abroad to Bruges and those sorts of places every year, and always dresses well, and gives quite nice luncheon-parties in the season. You can't do all that on two hundred a year, can you?"

"Does he write for any other papers?" queried Mrs. Troyle.

"No, you see he specializes so entirely on liturgy and ecclesiastical architecture that his field is rather restricted. He once tried the *Sporting and Dramatic* with an article on church edifices in famous fox-hunting centres, but it wasn't considered of sufficient general interest to be accepted. No, I don't see how he can support himself in his present style merely by what he writes."

"Perhaps he sells spurious transepts to American enthusiasts," suggested Clovis.

"How could you sell a transept?" said Mrs. Riversedge; "such a thing would be impossible."

"Whatever he may do to eke out his income," interrupted Mrs. Troyle, "he is certainly not going to fill in his leisure moments by making love to my maid."

"Of course not," agreed her hostess; "that must be put a stop to at once. But I don't quite know what we ought to do."

"You might put a barbed wire entanglement round the yew tree as a precautionary measure," said Clovis.

"I don't think that the disagreeable situation that has arisen is improved by flippancy," said Mrs. Riversedge; "a good maid is a treasure—"

"I am sure I don't know what I should do without Florinda," admitted Mrs. Troyle; "she understands my hair. I've long ago given up trying to do anything with it myself. I regard one's hair as I regard husbands: as long as one is seen together in public one's private divergences don't matter. Surely that was the luncheon gong."

Septimus Brope and Clovis had the smoking-room to themselves after lunch. The former seemed restless and preoccupied, the latter quietly observant.

"What is a lorry?" asked Septimus suddenly; "I don't mean the thing on wheels, of course I know what that is, but isn't there a bird with a name like that, the larger form of a lorikeet?"

"I fancy it's a lory, with one 'r,' " said Clovis lazily, "in which case it's no good to you."

Septimus Brope stared in some astonishment.

"How do you mean, no good to me?" he asked, with more than a trace of uneasiness in his voice.

"Won't rhyme with Florrie," explained Clovis briefly.

Septimus sat upright in his chair, with unmistakable alarm on his face.

"How did you find out? I mean how did you know I was trying to get a rhyme to Florrie?" he asked sharply.

"I didn't know," said Clovis, "I only guessed. When you wanted to turn the prosaic lorry of commerce into a feathered poem flitting through the verdure of a tropical forest, I knew you must be working up a sonnet, and Florrie was the only female name that suggested itself as rhyming with lorry."

Septimus still looked uneasy.

"I believe you know more," he said.

Clovis laughed quietly, but said nothing.

"How much do you know?" Septimus asked desperately.

"The yew tree in the garden," said Clovis.

"There! I felt certain I'd dropped it somewhere. But you must have guessed something before. Look here, you have surprised my secret. You won't give me away, will you? It is nothing to be ashamed of, but it wouldn't do for the editor of the *Cathedral Monthly* to go in openly for that sort of thing, would it?"

"Well, I suppose not," admitted Clovis.

"You see," continued Septimus, "I get quite a decent lot of money out of it. I could never live in the style I do on what I get as editor of the *Cathedral Monthly.* "

Clovis was even more startled than Septimus had been

earlier in the conversation, but he was better skilled in repressing surprise.

"Do you mean to say you get money out of—Florrie?" he asked.

"Not out of Florrie, as yet," said Septimus; "in fact, I don't mind saying that I'm having a good deal of trouble over Florrie. But there are a lot of others."

Clovis's cigarette went out.

"This is *very* interesting," he said slowly. And then, with Septimus Brope's next words, illumination dawned on him.

"There are heaps of others; for instance:

" 'Cora with the lips of coral,
You and I will never quarrel.'

"That was one of my earliest successes, and it still brings me in royalties. And then there is—'Esmeralda, when I first beheld her,' and 'Fair Teresa, how I love to please her,' both of those have been fairly popular. And there is one rather dreadful one," continued Septimus, flushing deep carmine, "which has brought me in more money than any of the others:

" 'Lively little Lucie
With her naughty *nez retrousse.'*

"Of course I loathe the whole lot of them; in fact, I'm rapidly becoming something of a woman-hater under their influence, but I can't afford to disregard the financial aspect of the matter. And at the same time you can understand that my position as an authority on ecclesiastical architecture and liturgical subjects would be weakened, if not altogether ruined, if it once got about that I was the author of 'Cora with the lips of coral' and all the rest of them."

Clovis had recovered sufficiently to ask in a sympathetic, if rather unsteady, voice what was the special trouble with "Florrie."

"I can't get her into lyric shape, try as I will," said Septimus mournfully. "You see, one has to work in a lot of sentimental, sugary compliment with a catchy rhyme, and a certain amount of personal biography or prophecy. They've all of them got to have a long string of past successes recorded about them, or else you've got to foretell blissful things about them and yourself in the future. For instance, there is:

> " 'Dainty little girlie Mavis,
> She is such a rara avis,
> All the money I can save is
> All to be for Mavis mine.'

"It goes to a sickening namby-pamby waltz tune, and for months nothing else was sung and hummed in Blackpool and other popular centres."

This time Clovis's self-control broke down badly.

"Please excuse me," he gurgled, "but I can't help it when I remember the awful solemnity of that article of yours that you so kindly read us last night, on the Coptic Church in its relation to early Christian worship."

Septimus groaned.

"You see how it would be," he said; "as soon as people knew me to be the author of that miserable sentimental twaddle, all respect for the serious labours of my life would be gone. I dare say I know more about memorial brasses than any one living, in fact I hope one day to publish a monograph on the subject, but I should be pointed out everywhere as the man whose ditties were in the mouths of minstrels along the entire coast-line of our Island home. Can you wonder that I positively hate Florrie all the time that I'm trying to grind out sugar-coated rhapsodies about her?"

"Why not give free play to your emotions, and be brutally abusive? An uncomplimentary refrain would have an instant success as a novelty if you were sufficiently outspoken."

"I've never thought of that," said Septimus, "and I'm afraid I couldn't break away from the habit of fulsome adulation and suddenly change my style."

"You needn't change your style in the least," said Clovis; "merely reverse the sentiment and keep to the inane phraseology of the thing. If you'll do the body of the song I'll knock off the refrain, which is the thing that principally matters, I believe. I shall charge half-shares in the royalties, and throw in my silence as to your guilty secret. In the eyes of the world you shall still be the man who has devoted his life to the study of transepts and Byzantine ritual; only sometimes, in the long winter evenings, when the wind howls drearily down the chimney and the rain beats against the windows, I shall think of you as the author of 'Cora with the lips of coral.' Of course, if in sheer gratitude at my silence you would like to take me for a much-needed holiday to the Adriatic or somewhere equally interesting, paying all expenses, I shouldn't dream of refusing."

Later in the afternoon Clovis found his aunt and Mrs. Riversedge indulging in gentle exercise in the Jacobean garden.

"I've spoken to Mr. Brope about F.," he announced.

"How splendid of you! What did he say?" came in a quick chorus from the two ladies.

"He was quite frank and straightforward with me when he saw that I knew his secret," said Clovis, "and it seems that his intentions were quite serious, if slightly unsuitable. I tried to show him the impracticability of the course that he was following. He said he wanted to be understood, and he seemed to think that Florinda would excel in that requirement, but I pointed out that there were probably dozens of delicately nurtured, purehearted young English girls who would be capable of understanding him, while Florinda was the only person in the world who understood my aunt's hair. That rather weighed with him, for he's not really a selfish animal, if you take him in the right way, and when I appealed to the memory of his happy childish days, spent amid the daisied fields of Leighton Buzzard (I suppose daisies do grow there), he was obviously affected. Anyhow, he gave me his word that he would put Florinda absolutely out of his mind, and he has agreed to go for a short trip abroad as the best distraction for his thoughts. I am going with him as far as Ragusa. If my aunt should wish to give me a really nice scarf-pin (to be chosen by myself), as a small recognition of the very considerable service I have done her, I shouldn't dream of refusing. I'm not one of those who think that because one is abroad one can go about dressed anyhow."

A few weeks later in Blackpool and places where they sing, the following refrain held undisputed sway:

> "How you bore me, Florrie,
> With those eyes of vacant blue;
> You'll be very sorry, Florrie,
> If I marry you.
> Though I'm easy-goin', Florrie,
> This I swear is true,
> I'll throw you down a quarry, Florrie,
> If I marry you."

THE BLUE-JAY YARN

A Story by Mark Twain

ANIMALS talk to each other, of course. There can be no question about that; but I suppose there are very few people who can understand them. I never knew but one man who could. I knew he could, however, because he told me so himself. He was a middle-aged, simple-hearted miner, who had lived in a lonely corner of California, among the woods and mountains, a good many years, and had studied the ways of his only neighbors, the beasts and the birds, until he believed he could accurately translate any remark which they made. This was Jim Baker. According to Jim Baker, some animals have only a limited education, and use only very simple words, and scarcely ever a comparison or a flowery figure; whereas, certain other animals have a large vocabulary, a fine command of language and a ready and fluent delivery—consequently these latter talk a great deal; they like it; they are conscious of their talent, and they enjoy "showing off." Baker said, that after long and careful observation, he had come to the conclusion that the blue-jays were the best talkers he had found among birds and beasts. Said he:

"There's more to a blue-jay than any other creature. He has got more moods and more different kinds of feelings than other creatures; and mind you, whatever a blue-jay feels, he can put into language. And no mere commonplace language, either, but rattling, out-and-out book-talk—

> *Mark Twain is the pen name of Samuel L. Clemens, whose stories capture forever the humor and fiber of life in the American Midwest in the 19th century.*

and bristling with metaphor, too—just bristling! And as for command of language—why you never see a blue-jay stuck for a word. No man ever did. They just boil out of him! And another thing: I've noticed a good deal, and there's no bird, or cow, or anything that uses as good grammar as a blue-jay. You may say a cat uses good grammar. Well, a cat does—but you let a cat get excited, once; you let a cat get to pulling fur with another cat on a shed, nights, and you'll hear grammar that will give you the lockjaw. Ignorant people think it's the *noise* which fighting cats make that is so aggravating, but it ain't so, it's the sickening grammar they use. Now I've never heard a jay use bad grammar but very seldom; and when they do, they are as ashamed as a human; they shut right down and leave.

"You may call a jay a bird. Well, so he is, in a measure—because he's got feathers on him, and don't belong to no church, perhaps; but otherwise he is just as much a human as you be. And I'll tell you for why. A jay's gifts, and instincts, and feelings, and interests, cover the whole ground. A jay hasn't got any more principle than a Congressman. A jay will lie, a jay will steal, a jay will deceive, a jay will betray; and four times out of five, a jay will go back on his solemnest promise. The sacredness of an obligation is a thing which you can't cram into no blue-jay's head. Now on top of all this, there's another thing: a jay can out-swear any gentleman in the mines. You think a cat can swear. Well, a cat can; but you give a blue-jay a subject that calls for his reserve-powers, and where is your cat? Don't talk to *me*—I know too much about this thing. And there's yet another thing: in the one little particular of scolding—just good, clean, out-and-out scolding—a blue-jay can lay over anything, human or divine. Yes, sir, a jay is everything that a man is. A jay can cry, a jay can laugh, a jay can feel shame, a jay can reason and plan and discuss, a jay likes gossip and scandal, a jay has got a sense of humor, a jay knows when he is an ass just as well as you do—maybe better. If a jay ain't human, he better take in his sign, that's all. Now I'm going to tell you a perfectly true fact about some blue-jays.

"When I first begun to understand jay language correctly, there was a little incident happened here. Seven years ago, the last man in this region but me, moved away. There stands his house—been empty ever since; a log house, with a plank roof—just one big room, and no more; no ceiling—nothing between the rafters and the floor. Well, one Sunday morning I was sitting out here in front of my cabin, with my cat, taking the sun, and looking at the blue hills, and listening to the leaves rustling so lonely in the trees, and thinking of the home away yonder in the States, that I hadn't heard from in thirteen years, when a blue-jay lit on that house, with an acorn in his mouth, and says, 'Hello, I reckon I've struck something!' When he spoke, the acorn dropped out of his mouth and rolled down the roof, of course, but he didn't care; his mind was all on the thing he had struck. It was a knot-hole in the roof. He cocked his head to one side, shut one eye and put the other one to the hole, like a 'possum looking down a jug; then he glanced up with his bright eyes, gave a wink or two with his wings—which signifies gratification, you understand—and says, 'It looks like a hole, it's located like a hole—blamed if I don't believe it is a hole!'

"Then he cocked his head down and took another look; he glances up perfectly joyful, this time; winks his wings and his tail both, and says, 'Oh, no, this ain't no fat thing, I reckon! If I ain't in luck!— why it's a perfectly elegant hole!' So he flew down and got that acorn, and fetched it up and dropped it in, and was just tilting his head back with the heavenliest smile on his face, when all of a sudden he was paralyzed into a listening attitude, and that smile faded gradually out of his countenance like breath off'n a razor, and the queerest look of surprise took its place. Then he says, 'Why I didn't hear it fall!' He cocked his eye at the hole again, and took a long look; raised up and shook his head; stepped around to the other side of the hole and took another look from that side; shook his head again. He studied a while, then he just went into the *details*—walked round and round the hole, and spied into it from every point of the compass. No use. Now he took a thinking attitude on the comb of the roof and scratched the back of his head with his right foot a minute, and finally says, "Well, it's too many for me, that's certain; must be a mighty long hole; however, I ain't got no time to fool around here, I got to 'tend to business; I reckon it's all right—chance it, anyway!'

"So he flew off and fetched another acorn and dropped it in, and tried to flirt his eye to the hole quick enough to see what become of it, but he was too late. He held his eye there as much as a minute; then he raised up and sighed, and says, 'Consound it, I don't seem to understand this thing, no way; however, I'll tackle her again.' He fetched another acorn and done his level best to see what become of it, but he couldn't. He says, 'Well, I never struck no such a hole as this before; I'm of the opinion it's a totally new kind of hole.' Then he begun to get mad. He held in for a spell, walking up and down the comb of the roof, and shaking his head and muttering to himself; but his feelings got the upper hand of him presently, and he broke loose and cussed himself black in the face. I never see a bird take on so about a little thing. When he got through he walks to the hole and looks in again for half a minute; then he says, 'Well, you're a long hole, and a deep hole, and a mighty singular hole altogether—but I've started to fill you, and I'm d—d if I *don't* fill you, if it takes a hundred years!'

"And with that, away he went. You never see a bird work so since you was born. He laid into his work, and the way he hove acorns into that hole for about two hours and a half was one of the most exciting and astonishing spectacles I ever struck. He never stopped to take a look any more—he just hove 'em in, and went for more. Well, at last he could hardly flop his wings, he was so tuckered out. He comes a-drooping down, once more, sweating like an ice-pitcher, drops his acorn in and says, 'Now I guess I've got the bulge on you by this time!' So he bent down for a look. If you'll believe me, when his head come up again he was just pale with rage. He says, 'I've shoveled acorns enough in there to keep the family thirty years, and if I can see a sign of one of 'em, I wish I may land in a museum with a belly full of sawdust in two minutes!'

"He just had strength enough to crawl up on to the comb and lean his back agin the chimbly, and then he collected his impressions and begun to free his mind. I see in a second that what I had mistook for profanity in the mines was only just the rudiments, as you may say.

"Another jay was going by, and heard him doing his devotions, and stops to inquire what was up. The sufferer told him the whole circumstances, and says, 'Now yonder's the hole, and if you don't believe me, go and look for yourself.' So this fellow went and looked, and comes back and says, 'How many did you say you put in there?' 'Not any less than two tons,' says the sufferer. The other jay went and looked again. He couldn't seem to make it out, so he raised a yell, and three more jays come. They all examined the hole, they all made the sufferer tell it over again, then they all discussed it, and got off as many leather-headed opinions about it as an average crowd of humans could have done.

"They called in more jays; then more and more, till pretty soon this whole region 'peared to have a blue flush about it. There must have been five thousand of them; and such another jawing and disputing and ripping and cussing, you never heard. Every jay in the whole lot put his eye to the hole, and delivered a more chuckled-headed opinion about the mystery than the jay that went there before him. They examined the house all over, too. The door was standing half-open, and at last one old jay happened to go and light on it and look in. Of course that knocked the mystery galley-west in a second. There lay the acorns, scattered all over the floor. He flopped his wings and raised a whoop. 'Come here!' he says, 'Come here, everybody; hang'd if this fool hasn't been trying to fill up a house with acorns!' They all came a-swooping down like a blue cloud, and as each fellow lit on the door and took a glance, the whole absurdity of the contract that the first jay had tackled hit him home and he fell over backwards suffocating with laughter, and the next jay took his place and done the same.

"Well, sir, they roosted around here on the house-top and the trees for an hour, and guffawed over that thing like human beings. It ain't any use to tell me a blue-jay hasn't got a sense of humor, because I know better. And memory too. They brought jays here from all over the United States to look down that hole, every summer for three years. Other birds too. And they could all see the point, except an owl that came from Nova Scotia to visit the Yo Semite, and he took this thing in on his way back. He said he couldn't see anything funny in it. But then, he was a good deal disappointed about Yo Semite, too."

THE GREY DUCKE

A Parody of Chaucer by Alexander Pope

WOMEN ben full of Ragerie,
Yet swinken not sans secresie
Thilke Moral shall ye understand,
From Schoole-boy's Tale of fayre Irelond:
Which to the Fennes hath him betake,
To filch the gray Ducke fro the Lake.
Right then, there passen by the Way
His Aunt, and eke her Daughters tway.
Ducke in his Trowses hath he hent,
Not to be spied of Ladies gent.
"But ho! our Nephew," (crieth one)
"Ho," quoth another, "Cozen John";
And stoppen, and laugh, and callen out,—
This sely Clerk full low doth lout:
They asken that, and talken this,
"Lo here is Coz, and here is Miss."
But, as he glozeth with Speeches soote,
The Ducke sore tickleth his Erse-root:
Fore-piece and buttons all-to-brest,
Forth thrust a white neck, and red crest.
"Te-he," cry'd Ladies; Clerke nought spake:
Miss star'd; and gray Ducke crieth Quake.
"O Moder, Moder" (quoth the daughter)
"Be thilke same thing Maids longen atter?
"Bette is to pyne on coals and chalke,
"Then trust on Mon, whose yerde can talke."

> *This parody is best if read aloud. Alexander Pope is
> one of the premier poets of the English language.*

A Genealogy of Etiquette

A Prejudice by H.L. Mencken

Barring sociology (which is yet, of course, scarcely a science at all, but rather a monkeyshine which happens to pay, like play-acting or theology), psychology is the youngest of the sciences, and hence chiefly guesswork, empiricism, hocus-pocus, poppycock. On the one hand, there are still enormous gaps in its data, so that the determination of its simplest principles remains difficult, not to say impossible; and, on the other hand, the very hollowness and nebulosity of it, particularly around its edges, encourages a horde of quacks to invade it, sophisticate it and make nonsense of it. Worse, this state of affairs tends to such confusion of effort and direction that the quack and the honest inquirer are often found in the same man. It is, indeed, a commonplace to encounter a professor who spends his days in the laborious accumulation of psychological statistics, sticking pins into babies and platting upon a chart the ebb and flow of their yells, and his nights chasing poltergeists and other such celestial fauna over the hurdles of a spiritualist's atelier, or gazing into a crystal in the privacy of his own chamber. The Binet test and the buncombe of mesmerism are alike the children of what we roughly denominate psychology, and perhaps of equal legitimacy. Even so ingenious and competent an investigator as Prof.

> *H.L. Mencken was editor of* The Baltimore Sun *and one of the most famous pundits of his day. He called his satires, written for* The Smart Set *magazine, Prejudices.*

Dr. Sigmund Freud, who has told us a lot that is of the first importance about the materials and machinery of thought, has also told us a lot that is trivial and dubious. The essential doctrines of Freudism, no doubt, come close to the truth, but many of Freud's remoter deductions are far more scandalous than sound, and many of the professed Freudians, both American and European, have grease-paint on their noses and bladders in their hands and are otherwise quite indistinguishable from evangelists and circus clowns.

In this condition of the science it is no wonder that we find it wasting its chief force upon problems that are petty and idle when they are not downright and palpably insoluble, and passing over problems that are of immediate concern to all of us, and that might be quite readily solved, or, at any rate, considerably illuminated, by an intelligent study of the data already available. After all, not many of us care a hoot whether Sir Oliver Lodge and the Indian chief Wok-a-wok-a-mok are happy in heaven, for not many of us have any hope or desire to meet them there. Nor are we greatly excited by the discovery that, of twenty-five freshmen who are hit with clubs, $17\,^3/_4$ will say "Ouch!" and $22\,^1/_5$ will say "Damn!"; nor by a table showing that 38.2 per centum of all men accused of homicide confess when locked up with the carcasses of their victims, including 23.4 per centum who are innocent; nor by plans and specifications, by Cagliostro out of Lucrezia Borgia, for teaching poor, Godforsaken school children to write before they can read and to multiply before they can add; nor by endless disputes between half-witted pundits as to the precise difference between perception and cognition; nor by even longer feuds, between pundits even crazier, over free will, the subconscious, the endoneurium, the functions of the corpora quadrigemina, and the meaning of dreams in which one is pursued by hyenas, process-servers or grass-widows.

Nay; we do not bubble with rejoicing when such fruits of psychological deep-down-diving and much-mud upbringing researches are laid before us, for after all they do not offer us any nourishment, there is nothing in them to engage our teeth, they fail to make life more comprehensible, and hence more bearable. What we yearn to know something about is the process whereby the ideas of everyday are engendered in the skulls of those about us, to the end that we may pursue a straighter and a safer course through the muddle that is life. Why do the great majority of Presbyterians (and, for that matter, of Baptists, Episcopalians, and Swedenborgians as well) regard it as unlucky to meet a black cat and lucky to find a pin? What are the logical steps behind the theory that it is indecent to eat peas with a knife? By what process does an otherwise sane man arrive at the conclusion that he will go to hell unless he is baptized by total immersion in water? What causes men to be faithful to their wives: habit, fear, poverty, lack of imagination, lack of enterprise, stupidity, religion? What is the psychological basis of commercial morality? What is the true nature of the vague pooling of desires that Rousseau called the social contract? Why does an American regard it as scandalous to wear dress clothes at a funeral, and a Frenchman regard it as equally scandalous *not* to wear them? Why is it that men trust one another so readily, and women trust one another so seldom? Why are we all so greatly affected by statements that we know are not true?— *e.g.* in Lincoln's Gettysburg speech, the Declaration of Independence and the CIII Psalm. What is the origin of the so-called double standard of morality? Why are women forbidden to take off their hats in church? What is happiness? Intelligence? Sin? Courage? Virtue? Beauty?

All these are questions of interest and importance to all of us, for their solution would materially improve the accuracy of our outlook upon the world, and with it our mastery of our environment, but the psychologists, busily engaged in chasing their tails, leave them unanswered, and, in most cases, even unasked. The late William James, more acute than the general, saw how precious little was known about the psychological inwardness of religion, and to the illumination of this darkness he addressed himself in his book, *The Varieties of Religious Experience*. But life being short and science long, he got little beyond the statement of the problem and the marshaling of the grosser evidence—and even at this business he allowed himself to be constantly interrupted by spooks, hobgoblins, seventh sons of seventh sons and other such characteristic pets of psychologists. In the same way one Gustav le Bon, a Frenchman, undertook a psychological study of the crowd mind—and then blew up. Add the investigations of Freud and his school, chiefly into abnormal states of mind, and those of Lombroso and his school, chiefly quackish and for the yellow journals, and the idle romancing of such inquirers as Prof. Dr. Thorstein Veblen, and you have exhausted the list of contributions to what may be called practical and everyday psychology. The rev. professors, I daresay, have been doing some useful plowing and planting. All of their meticulous pin-sticking and measuring and chart making, in the course of time, will enable their successors to approach the real problems of mind with more assurance than is now possible, and perhaps help to their solution. But in the meantime the public and social utility of psychology remains very small, for it is still unable to differentiate accurately between the true and the false, or to give us any effective protection against the fallacies, superstitions, crazes and hysterias which rage in the world.

In this emergency it is not only permissible but even laudable for the amateur to sniff inquiringly through the psychological pasture, essaying modestly to uproot things that the myopic (or, perhaps more accurately, hypermetropic) professionals have overlooked. The late Friedrich Wilhelm Nietzsche did it often, and the usufructs were many curious and daring guesses, some of them probably close to accuracy, as to the genesis of this, that or the other common delusion of man—*i.e.,* the delusion that the law of the survival of the fittest may be repealed by an act of Congress. Into the same field several very interesting expeditions have been made by Dr. Elsie Clews Parsons, a lady once celebrated by Park Row for her invention of trial marriage—an invention, by the way, in which the Nietzsche aforesaid preceded her by at least a dozen years. The records of her researches are to be found in a brief series of books: "The Family," "The Old-Fashioned Woman" and "Fear and Conventionality." Apparently they have wrung relatively little esteem from the learned, for I seldom encounter a reference to them, and Dr. Parsons herself is denied the very modest reward of mention in "Who's Who in America." Nevertheless, they are extremely instructive books, particularly "Fear and Conventionality." I know of no other work, indeed, which offers a better array of observations upon that powerful complex of assumptions, prejudices, instinctive reactions, racial emotions and unbreakable vices of mind which enters so massively into the daily thinking of all of us. The author does not concern herself, as so many psychologists fall into the habit of doing, with thinking as a purely laboratory phenomenon, a process in vacuo. What she deals with is thinking as it is done by men and women in the real world—thinking that is only half intellectual, the other half being as automatic and unintelligent as swallowing, blinking the eye or falling in love.

It is the business of Dr. Parsons, in "Fear and Conventionality," to prod into certain of the ideas which thus pour into every man's mind from the circumambient air, sweeping away, like some huge cataract, the feeble resistance that his own powers of ratiocination can offer. In particular, she devotes herself to an examination of those general ideas which condition the thought and action of man as a social being—those general ideas which govern his everyday attitude toward his fellow-men and his prevailing view of himself. In one direction they lay upon us the bonds of what we call etiquette, *i.e.*, the duty of considering the habits and feelings of those around us—and in another direction they throttle us with what we call morality—*i.e.,* the rules which protect the life and property of those around us. But, as Dr. Parsons shows, the boundary between etiquette and morality is very dimly drawn, and it is often impossible to say of a given action whether it is downright immoral or merely a breach of the punctilio. Even when the moral law is plainly running, considerations of mere amenity and politeness may still make themselves felt. Thus, as Dr. Parsons points out, there is even an etiquette of adultery. "The *ami de la famille* vows not to kiss his mistress in her husband's house"—not in fear, but "as an expression of conjugal consideration," as a sign that he has not forgotten the thoughtfulness expected of a gentleman. And in this delicate field, as might be expected, the differences in racial attitudes are almost diametrical. The Englishman, surprising his wife with a lover, sues the rogue for damages and has public opinion behind him, but for an American to do it would be for him to lose caste at once and forever. The plain and only duty of the American is to open upon the fellow with artillery, hitting him if the scene is south of the Potomac and missing him if it is above.

I confess to an endless interest in such puzzling niceties, and to much curiosity as to their origins and meaning. Why do we Americans take off our hats when we meet a flapper on the street, and yet stand covered before a male of the highest eminence? A Continental would regard this last as boorish to the last degree; in greeting any equal or superior, male or female, actual or merely conventional, he lifts his head-piece. Why does it strike us as ludicrous to see a man in dress clothes before 6 P.M.? The Continental puts them on whenever he has a solemn visit to make, whether the hour be six or noon. Why do we regard it as indecent to tuck the napkin between the waistcoat buttons—or into the neck!—at meals? The Frenchman does it without thought of crime. So does the Italian. So does the German. All three are punctilious men—far more so, indeed, than we are. Why do we snicker at the man who wears a wedding ring? Most Continentals would stare askance at the husband who didn't. Why is it bad manners in Europe and America to ask a stranger his or her age, and a friendly attention in China? Why do we regard it as absurd to distinguish a woman by her husband's title—*e.g.,* Mrs. Judge Jones, Mrs. Professor Smith? In Teutonic and Scandinavian Europe the omission of the title would be looked upon as an affront.

Such fine distinctions, so ardently supported, raise many interesting questions, but the attempt to answer them quickly gets one bogged. Several years ago I ventured to lift a sad voice against a custom common in America: that of married men, in speaking of their wives, employing the full panoply of "Mrs. Brown." It was my contention—supported, I thought, by logical considerations of the loftiest order—that a husband, in speaking of his wife to his equals, should say "my wife"—that the more formal mode of designation should be reserved for inferiors and for strangers of undetermined position. This contention, somewhat to my surprise, was vigorously combated by various volunteer experts. At first they rested their case upon the mere authority of custom, forgetting that this custom was by no means universal. But finally one of them came forward with a more analytical and cogent defense—the defense, to wit, that "my wife" connoted proprietorship and was thus offensive to a wife's *amour propre*. But what of "my sister" and "my mother"? Surely it is nowhere the custom for a man, addressing an equal, to speak of his sister as "Miss Smith." The discussion, however, came to nothing. It was impossible to carry it on logically. The essence of all such inquiries lies in the discovery that there is a force within the liver and lights of man that is infinitely more potent than logic. His reflections, perhaps, may take on intellectually recognizable forms, but they seldom lead to intellectually recognizable conclusions.

Nevertheless, Dr. Parsons offers something in her book that may conceivably help to a better understanding of them, and that is the doctrine that the strange persistence of these rubber-stamp ideas, often unintelligible and sometimes plainly absurd, is due to fear, and that this fear is the product of a very real danger. The safety of human society lies in the assumption that every individual composing it, in a given situation, will act in a manner hitherto approved as seemly. That is to say, he is expected to react to his environment according to a fixed pattern, not necessarily because that pattern is the best imaginable, but simply because it is determined and understood. If he fails to do so, if he reacts in a novel manner—conducive, perhaps, to his better advantage or to what he thinks is his better advantage—then he disappoints the expectation of those around him, and forces them to meet the new situation he has created by the exercise of independent thought. Such independent thought, to a good many men, is quite impossible, and to the overwhelming majority of men, extremely painful. "To all of us," says Dr. Parsons, "to the animal, to the savage and to the civilized being, few demands are as uncomfortable, ... disquieting or fearful, as the call to innovate.... Adaptations we all of us dislike or hate. We dodge or shirk them as best we may." And the man who compels us to make them against our wills we punish by withdrawing from him that understanding and friendliness which he, in turn, looks for and counts upon. In other words, we set him apart as one who is anti-social and not to be dealt with, and according as his rebellion has been small or great, we call him a boor or a criminal.

This distrust of the unknown, this fear of doing something unusual, is probably at the bottom of many ideas and institutions that are commonly credited to other motives. For example, monogamy. The orthodox explanation of monogamy is that it is a manifestation of the desire to have and to hold property—that the husband defends his solitary right to his wife, even at the cost of his own freedom, because she is the pearl among his chattels. But Dr. Parsons argues, and with a good deal of plausibility, that the real moving force, both in the husband and the wife, may be merely the force of habit, the antipathy to experiment and innovation. It is easier and safer to stick to the one wife than to risk adventures with another wife—and the immense social pressure that I have just described is all on the side of sticking. Moreover, the indulgence of a habit automatically strengthens its bonds. What we have done once or thought once, we are more apt than we were before to do and think again. Or, as the late Prof. William James put it, "the selection of a particular hole to live in, of a particular mate, . . . a particular anything, in short, out of a possible multitude . . . carries with it an insensibility to *other* opportunities and occasions—an insensibility which can only be described physiologically as an inhibition of new impulses by the habit of old ones already formed. The possession of homes and wives of our own makes us strangely insensible to the charms of other people.... The original impulse which got us homes, wives, . . . seems to exhaust itself in its first achievements and to leave no surplus energy for reacting on new cases." Thus the benedict looks no more on women (at least for a while), and the post-honeymoon bride, as the late David Graham Phillips once told us, neglects the bedizenments which got her a man.

In view of the popular or general character of most of the taboos which put a brake upon personal liberty in thought and action—that is to say, in view of their enforcement by people in the mass, and not by definite specialists in conduct—it is quite natural to find that they are of extra force in democratic societies, for it is the distinguishing mark of democratic societies that they exalt the powers of the majority almost infinitely, and tend to deny the minority any rights whatever. Under a society dominated by a small caste the revolutionist in custom, despite the axiom to the contrary, has a relatively easy time of it, for the persons whose approval he seeks for his innovation are relatively few in number, and most of them are already habituated to more or less intelligible and independent thinking. But under a democracy he is opposed by a horde so vast that it is a practical impossibility for him, without complex and expensive machinery, to reach and convince all of its members, and even if he could reach them he would find most of them quite incapable of rising out of their accustomed grooves. They cannot understand innovations that are genuinely novel and they don't want to understand them; their one desire is to put them down. Even at this late day, with enlightenment raging through the republic like a pestilence, it would cost the average Southern or Middle Western Congressman his seat if he appeared among his constituents in spats, or wearing a wrist-watch. And if a Justice of the Supreme Court of the United States, however gigantic his learning and his juridic rectitude, were taken in crim. con. with the wife of a Senator, he would be destroyed instanter. And if, suddenly revolting against the democratic idea, he were to propose, however gingerly, its abandonment, he would be destroyed with the same dispatch.

But here I wander into political speculation and no doubt stand in contumacy of some statute of Congress. Dr. Parsons avoids politics in her very interesting book. She confines herself to the purely social relations, *e.g.,* between man and woman, parent and child, host and guest, master and servant. The facts she offers are vastly interesting, and their discovery and coordination reveal a tremendous industry, but of even greater interest are the facts that lie over the margin of her inquiry. Here is a golden opportunity for other investigators: I often wonder that the field is so little explored. Perhaps the Freudians, once they get rid of their sexual obsession, will enter it and chart it. No doubt the inferiority complex described by Prof. Dr. Alfred Adler will one day provide an intelligible explanation of many of the puzzling phenomena of mob thinking. In the work of Prof. Dr. Freud himself there is, perhaps, a clew to the origin and anatomy of Puritanism, that worst of intellectual nephritises. I live in hope that the Freudians will fall upon the business without much further delay. What is the genesis of the American axiom that the fine arts are unmanly? What is the precise machinery of the process called falling in love? Why do people believe newspapers?

Let there be light!

CIRCLES

An Essay by Ralph Waldo Emerson

> Nature centres into balls,
> And her proud ephemerals,
> Fast to surface and outside,
> Scan the profile of the sphere;
> Knew they what that signified,
> A new genesis were here.

The eye is the first circle; the horizon which it forms is the second; and throughout nature this primary picture is repeated without end. It is the highest emblem in the cipher of the world. St. Augustine described the nature of God as a circle whose centre was everywhere and its circumference nowhere. We are all our lifetime reading the copious sense of this first of forms. One moral we have already deduced in considering the circular or compensatory character of every human action. Another analogy we shall now trace, that every action admits of being outdone. Our life is an apprenticeship to the truth that around every circle another can be drawn; that there is no end in nature, but every end is a beginning; that there is always another dawn risen on mid-noon, and under every deep a lower deep opens.

> *Ralph Waldo Emerson, the great Transcendentalist, is naturally heads and shoulders above the madding crowd—which is to say he could run circles around us all. His is a voice which must not be silenced.*

This fact, as far as it symbolizes the moral fact of the Unattainable, the flying Perfect, around which the hands of man can never meet, at once the inspirer and the condemner of every success, may conveniently serve us to connect many illustrations of human power in every department.

There are no fixtures in nature. The universe is fluid and volatile. Permanence is but a word of degrees. Our globe seen by God is a transparent law, not a mass of facts. The law dissolves the fact and holds it fluid. Our culture is the predominance of an idea which draws after it all this train of cities and institutions. Let us rise into another idea; they will disappear. The Greek sculpture is all melted away, as if it had been statues of ice: here and there a solitary figure or fragment remaining, as we see flecks and scraps of snow left in cold dells and mountain clefts in June and July. For the genius that created it creates now somewhat else. The Greek letters last a little longer, but are already passing under the same sentence and tumbling into the inevitable pit which the creation of new thought opens for all that is old. The new continents are built out of the ruins of an old planet; the new races fed out of the decomposition of the foregoing. New arts destroy the old. See the investment of capital in aqueducts, made useless by hydraulics; fortifications, by gunpowder; roads and canals, by railways; sails, by steam; steam, by electricity.

You admire this tower of granite, weathering the hurts of so many ages. Yet a little waving hand built this huge wall, and that which builds is better than that which is built. The hand that built can topple it down much faster. Better than the hand and nimbler was the invisible thought which wrought through it; and thus ever, behind the coarse effect, is a fine cause, which, being narrowly seen, is itself the effect of a finer cause. Every thing looks permanent until its secret is known. A rich estate appears to women and children a firm and lasting fact; to a merchant, one easily created out of any materials, and easily lost. An orchard, good tillage, good grounds, seem a fixture, like a gold mine, or a river, to a citizen; but to a large farmer, not much more fixed than the state of the crop. Nature looks provokingly stable and secular, but it has a cause like all the rest; and when once I comprehend that, will these fields stretch so immovably wide, these leaves hang so individually considerable? Permanence is a word of degrees. Everything is medial. Moons are no more bounds to spiritual power than bat-balls.

The key to every man is his thought. Sturdy and defying though he look, he has a helm which he obeys, which is the idea after which all his facts are classified. He can only be reformed by showing him a new idea which commands his own. The life of man is a self-evolving circle, which, from a ring imperceptibly small, rushes on all sides outwards to new and larger circles, and that without end. The extent to which this generation of circles, wheel without wheel, will go, depends on the force of truth of the individual soul. For it is the inert effort of each thought, having formed itself into a circular wave of circumstance, as for instance an empire, rules of an art, a local usage, a religious rite, to heap itself on that ridge and to solidify and hem in the life. But if the soul is quick and strong it bursts over that boundary on all sides and expands another orbit on the great deep, which also runs up into a high wave, with attempt again to stop and to bind. But the heart refuses to be imprisoned; in its first and narrowest pulses it already tends outward with a vast force and to immense and innumerable expansions.

Every ultimate fact is only the first of a new series. Every general law only a particular fact of some more general law presently to disclose itself. There is no outside, no inclosing wall, no circumference to us. The man finishes his story—how good! how final! how it puts a new face on all things! He fills the sky. Lo, on the other side rises also a man and draws a circle around the circle we had just pronounced the outline of the sphere. Then already is our first speaker not man, but only a first speaker. His only redress is forthwith to draw a circle outside of his antagonist. And so men do by themselves. The result of to-day, which haunts the mind and cannot be escaped, will presently be abridged into a word, and the principle that seemed to explain nature will itself be included as one example of a bolder generalization. In the thought of to-morrow there is a power to upheave all thy creed, all the creeds, all the literatures of the nations, and marshal thee to a heaven which no epic dream has yet depicted. Every man is not so much a workman in the world as he is a suggestion of that he should be. Men walk as prophecies of the next age.

Step by step we scale this mysterious ladder; the steps are actions, the new prospect is power. Every several result is threatened and judged by that which follows. Every one seems to be contradicted by the new; it is only limited by the new. The new statement is always hated by the old, and, to those dwelling in the old, comes like an abyss of scepticism. But the eye soon gets wonted to it, for the eye and it are effects of one cause; then its innocency and benefit appear, and presently, all its energy spent, it pales and dwindles before the revelation of the new hour.

Fear not the new generalization. Does the fact look crass and material, threatening to degrade thy theory of spirit? Resist it not; it goes to refine and raise thy theory of matter just as much.

There are no fixtures to men, if we appeal to consciousness. Every man supposes himself not to be fully understood; and if there is any truth in him, if he rests at last on the divine soul, I see not how it can be otherwise. The last chamber, the last closet, he must feel was never opened; there is always a residuum unknown, unanalyzable. That is, every man believes that he has a greater possibility.

Our moods do not believe in each other. To-day I am full of thoughts and can write what I please. I see no reason why I should not have the same thought, the same power of expression, to-morrow. What I write, whilst I write it, seems the most natural thing in the world: but yesterday I saw a dreary vacuity in this direction in which now I see so much; and a month hence, I doubt not, I shall wonder who he was that wrote so many continuous pages. Alas for this infirm faith, this will not strenuous, this vast ebb of a vast flow! I am God in nature; I am a weed by the wall.

The continual effort to raise himself above himself, to work a pitch above his last height, betrays itself in a man's relations. We thirst for approbation, yet cannot forgive the approver. The sweet of nature is love; yet if I have a friend I am tormented by my imperfections. The love of me accuses the other party. If he were high enough to slight me, then could I love him, and rise by my affection to new heights. A man's growth is seen in the successive choirs of his friends. For every friend whom he loses for truth, he gains a better. I thought as I walked in the woods and mused on my friends, why should I play with them this game of idolatry? I know and see too well, when not voluntarily blind, the speedy limits of persons called high and worthy. Rich, noble and great they are by the liberality of our speech, but truth is sad. O blessed Spirit, whom I forsake for these, they are not thee! Every personal consideration that we allow costs us heavenly state. We sell the thrones of angels for a short and turbulent pleasure.

How often must we learn this lesson? Men cease to interest us when we find their limitations. The only sin is limitation. As soon as you once come up with a man's limitations, it is all over with him. Has he talents? has he enterprises? has he knowledge? It boots not. Infinitely alluring and attractive was he to you yesterday, a great hope, a sea to swim in; now, you have found his shores, found it a pond, and you care not if you never see it again.

Each new step we take in thought reconciles twenty seemingly discordant facts, as expressions of one law

Aristotle and Plato are reckoned the respective heads of two schools. A wise man will see that Aristotle Platonizes. By going one step farther back in thought, discordant opinions are reconciled by being seen to be two extremes of one principle, and we can never go so far back as to preclude a still higher vision.

Beware when the great God lets loose a thinker on this planet. Then all things are at risk. It is as when a conflagration has broken out in a great city, and no man knows what is safe, or where it will end. There is not a piece of science but its flank may be turned to-morrow; there is not any literary reputation, not the so-called eternal names of fame, that may not be revised and condemned. The very hopes of man, the thoughts of his heart, the religion of nations, the manners and morals of mankind are all at the mercy of a new generalization. Generalization is always a new influx of the divinity into the mind. Hence the thrill that attends it.

Valor consists in the power of self-recovery, so that a man cannot have his flank turned, cannot be out-generalled, but put him where you will, he stands. This can only be by his preferring truth to his past apprehension of truth, and his alert acceptance of it from whatever quarter; the intrepid conviction that his laws, his relations to society, his Christianity, his world, may at any time be superseded and decease.

There are degrees in idealism. We learn first to play with it academically, as the magnet was once a toy. Then we see in the heyday of youth and poetry that it may be true, that it is true in gleams and fragments. Then, its countenance waxes stern and grand, and we see that it must be true. It now shows itself ethical and practical. We learn that God *is;* that he is in me; and that all things are shadows of him. The idealism of Berkeley is only a crude statement of the idealism of Jesus, and that again is a crude statement of the fact that all nature is the rapid efflux of goodness executing and organizing itself. Much more obviously is history and the state of the world at any one time directly dependent on the intellectual classification then existing in the minds of men. The things which are dear to men at this hour are so on account of the ideas which have emerged on their mental horizon, and which cause the present order of things, as a tree bears its apples. A new degree of culture would instantly revolutionize the entire system of human pursuits.

Conversation is a game of circles. In conversation we pluck up the *termini* which bound the common of silence on every side. The parties are not to be judged by the spirit they partake and even express under this Pentecost. Tomorrow they will have receded from this high-watermark. Tomorrow you shall find them stooping under the old packsaddles. Yet let us enjoy the cloven flame whilst it glows on our walls. When each new speaker strikes a new light, emancipates us from the oppression of the last speaker to oppress us with the greatness and exclusiveness of his own thought, then yields us to another redeemer, we seem to recover our rights, to become men. O, what truths profound and executable only in ages and orbs, are supposed in the announcement of every truth! In common hours, society sits cold and statuesque. We all stand waiting, empty—knowing, possibly, that we can be full, surrounded by mighty symbols which are not symbols to us, but prose and trivial toys. Then cometh the god and converts the statues into fiery men, and by a flash of his eye burns up the veil which shrouded all things, and the meaning of the very furniture, of cup and saucer, of chair and clock and tester, is manifest. The facts which loomed so large in the fogs of yesterday—property, climate, breeding, personal beauty and the like, have strangely changed their proportions. All that we reckoned settled shakes and rattles; and literatures, cities, climates, religions, leave their foundations and dance before our eyes. And yet here again see the swift circumscription! Good as is discourse, silence is better, and shames it. The length of the discourse indicates the distance of thought betwixt the speaker and the hearer. If they were at a perfect understanding in any part, no words would be necessary thereon. If at one in all parts, no words would be suffered.

Literature is a point outside of our hodiernal circle through which a new one may be described. The use of literature is to afford us a platform whence we may command a view of our present life, a purchase by which we may move it. We fill ourselves with ancient learning, install ourselves the best we can in Greek, in Punic, in Roman houses, only that we may wiselier see French, English and American houses and modes of living. In like manner we see literature best from the midst of wild nature, or from the din of affairs, or from a high religion. The field cannot be well seen from within the field. The astronomer must have his diameter of the earth's orbit as a base to find the parallax of any star.

Therefore we value the poet. All the argument and all the wisdom is not in the encyclopædia, or the treatise on metaphysics, or the Body of Divinity, but in the sonnet or the play. In my daily work I incline to repeat my old steps, and do not believe in remedial force, in the power of change and reform. But some Petrarch or Ariosto, filled with the new wine of his imagination, writes me an ode or a brisk romance, full of daring thought and action. He smites and arouses me with his shrill tones, breaks up my whole chain of habits, and I open my eye on my own possibilities. He claps wings to the sides of all the solid old lumber of the world, and I am capable once more of choosing a straight path in theory and practice.

We have the same need to command a view of the religion of the world. We can never see Christianity from the catechism:—from the pastures, from a boat in the pond, from amidst the songs of wood-birds we possibly may. Cleansed by the elemental light and wind, steeped in the sea of beautiful forms which the field offers us, we may chance to cast a right glance back upon biography. Christianity is rightly dear to the best of mankind; yet was there never a young philosopher whose breeding had fallen into the Christian church by whom that brave text of Paul's was not specially prized, "Then shall also the Son be subject unto Him who put all things under him, that God may be all in all." Let the claims and virtues of persons be never so great and welcome the instinct of man presses eagerly onward to the impersonal and illimitable, and gladly arms itself against the dogmatism of bigots with this generous word out of the book itself.

The natural world may be conceived of as a system of concentric circles, and we now and then detect in nature slight dislocations which apprize us that this surface on which we now stand is not fixed, but sliding. These manifold tenacious qualities, this chemistry and vegetation, these metals and animals, which seem to stand there for their own sake, are means and methods only, are words of God, and as fugitive as other words. Has the naturalist or chemist learned his craft, who has explored the gravity of atoms and the elective affinities, who has not yet discerned the deeper law whereof this is only a partial or approximate statement, namely that like draws to like, and that the goods which belong to you gravitate to you and need not be pursued with pains and cost? Yet is that statement approximate also, and not final. Omnipresence is a higher fact. Not through subtle subterranean channels need friend and fact be drawn to their counterpart, but, rightly considered, these things proceed from the eternal generation of the soul. Cause and effect are two sides of one fact.

The same law of eternal procession ranges all that we call the virtues, and extinguishes each in the light of a better. The great man will not be prudent in the popular sense; all his prudence will be so much deduction from his grandeur. But it behoves each to see, when he sacrifices prudence, to what god he devotes it; if to ease and pleasure, he had better be prudent still; if to a great trust, he can well spare his mule and panniers who has a winged chariot instead. Geoffrey draws on his boots to go through the woods, that his feet may be safer from the bite of snakes; Aaron never thinks of such a peril. In many years neither is harmed by such an accident. Yet it seems to me that with every precaution you take against such an evil you put yourself into the power of the evil. I suppose that the highest prudence is the lowest prudence. Is this too sudden a rushing from the centre to the verge of our orbit? Think how many times we shall fall back into pitiful calculations before we take up our rest in the great sentiment, or make the verge of to-day the new centre. Besides, your bravest sentiment is familiar to the humblest men. The poor and the low have their way of expressing the last facts of philosophy as well as you. "Blessed be nothing" and "The worse things are, the better they are" are proverbs which express the transcendentalism of common life.

One man's justice is another's injustice; one man's beauty another's ugliness; one man's wisdom another's folly; as one beholds the same objects from a higher point of view. One man thinks Justice consists in paying debts, and has no measure in his abhorrence of another who is very remiss in this duty and makes the creditor wait tediously. But that second man has his own way of looking at things; asks himself which debt must I pay first, the debt to the rich, or the debt to the poor? the debt of money, or the debt of thought to mankind, of genius to nature? For you, O broker, there is no other principle but arithmetic. For me, commerce is of trivial import; love, faith, truth of character, the aspiration of man, these are sacred; nor can I detach one duty, like you, from all other duties, and concentrate my forces mechanically on the payment of moneys. Let me live onward; you shall find that, though slower, the progress of my character will liquidate all these debts without injustice to higher claims. If a man should dedicate himself to the payment of notes, would not this be injustice? Owes he no debt but money? And are all claims on him to be postponed to a land-lord's or a banker's?

There is no virtue which is final; all are initial. The virtues of society are vices of the saint. The terror of reform is the discovery that we must cast away our virtues, or what we have always esteemed such, into the same pit that has consumed our grosser vices.

> "Forgive his crimes, forgive his virtues too,
> Those smaller faults, half converts to the right."
> —Edward Young, *Night Thoughts*

It is the highest power of divine moments that they abolish our contritions also. I accuse myself of sloth and unprofitableness day by day; but when these waves of God flow into me I no longer reckon lost time. I no longer poorly compute my possible achievement by what remains to me of the month or the year; for these moments confer a sort of omnipresence and omnipotence which asks nothing of duration, but sees that the energy of the mind is commensurate with the work to be done, without time.

And thus, O circular philosopher, I hear some reader exclaim, you have arrived at a fine Pyrrhonism, at an equivalence and indifferency of all actions, and would fain teach us that *if we are true,* forsooth, our crimes may be lively stones out of which we shall construct the temple of the true God.

I am not careful to justify myself. I own I am gladdened by seeing the predominance of the saccharine principle throughout vegetable nature, and not less by beholding in morals that unrestrained inundation of the principle of good into every chink and hole that selfishness has left open, yea into selfishness and sin itself; so that no evil is pure, nor hell itself without its extreme satisfactions. But lest I should mislead any when I have my own head and obey my whims, let me remind the reader that I am only an experimenter. Do not set the least value on what I do, or the least discredit on what I do not, as if I pretended to settle any thing as true or false. I unsettle all things. No facts are to me sacred; none are profane; I simply experiment, an endless seeker with no Past at my back.

Yet this incessant movement and progression which all things partake could never become sensible to us but by contrast to some principle of fixture or stability in the soul. Whilst the eternal generation of circles proceeds, the eternal generator abides. That central life is somewhat superior to creation, superior to knowledge and thought, and contains all its circles. Forever it labors to create a life and thought as large and excellent as itself; but in vain; for that which is made instructs how to make a better.

Thus there is no sleep, no pause, no preservation, but all things renew, germinate and spring. Why should we import rags and relics into the new hour? Nature abhors the old, and old age seems the only disease: others run into this one. We call it by many names—fever, intemperance, insanity, stupidity and crime: they are all forms of old age: they are rest, conservatism, appropriation, inertia; not newness, not the way onward. We grizzle every day. I see no need of it. Whilst we converse with what is above us, we do not grow old, but grow young. Infancy, youth, receptive, aspiring, with religious eye looking upward, counts itself nothing and abandons itself to the instruction flowing from all sides. But the man and woman of seventy assume to know all; throw up their hope; renounce aspiration; accept the actual for the necessary and talk down to the young. Let them then become organs of the Holy Ghost; let them be lovers; let them behold truth; and their eyes are uplifted, their wrinkles smoothed, they are perfumed again with hope and power. This old age ought not to creep on a human mind. In nature every moment is new; the past is always swallowed and forgotten; the coming only is sacred. Nothing is secure but life, transition, the energizing spirit. No love can be bound by oath or covenant to secure it against a higher love. No truth so sublime but it may be trivial to-morrow in the light of new thoughts. People wish to be settled: only as far as they are unsettled is there any hope for them.

Life is a series of surprises. We do not guess to-day the mood, the pleasure, the power of to-morrow, when we are building up our being. Of lower states—of acts of routine and sense, we can tell somewhat, but the masterpieces of God, the total growths and universal movements of the soul, he hideth; they are incalculable. I can know that truth is divine and helpful; but how it shall help me I can have no guess, for *so to be* is the sole inlet of *so to know*. The new position of the advancing man has all the powers of the old, yet has them all new. It carries in its bosom all the energies of the past, yet is itself an exhalation of the morning. I cast away in this new moment all my once hoarded knowledge, as vacant and vain. Now for the first time seem I to know any thing rightly. The simplest words—we do not know what they mean except when we love and aspire.

The difference between talents and character is adroitness to keep the old and trodden round, and power and courage to make a new road to new and better goals. Character makes an overpowering present, a cheerful, determined hour, which fortifies all the company by making them see that much is possible and excellent that was not thought of. Character dulls the impression of particular events. When we see the conqueror we do not think much of any one battle or success. We see that we had exaggerated the difficulty. It was easy to him. The great man is not convulsible or tormentable. He is so much that events pass over him without much impression. People say sometimes, "See what I have overcome; see how cheerful I am; see how completely I have triumphed over these black events." Not if they still remind me of the black event—they have not yet conquered. Is it conquest to be a gay and decorated sepulchre, or a half-crazed widow, hysterically laughing? True conquest is the causing the black event to fade and disappear as an early cloud of insignificant result in a history so large and advancing.

The one thing which we seek with insatiable desire is to forget ourselves, to be surprised out of our propriety, to lose our sempiternal memory and to do something without knowing how or why; in short to draw a new circle. Nothing great was ever achieved without enthusiasm. The way of life is wonderful. It is by abandonment. The great moments of history are the facilities of performance through the strength or ideas, as the works of genius and religion. "A man," said Oliver Cromwell, "never rises so high as when he knows not whither he is going." Dreams and drunkenness, the use of opium and alcohol are the semblance and counterfeit of this oracular genius, and hence their dangerous attraction for men. For the like reason they ask the aid of wild passions, as in gaming and war, to ape in some manner these flames and generosities of the heart.

THE STAR

A Story by H.G. Wells

It was on the first day of the new year that the announcement was made, almost simultaneously from three observatories, that the motion of the planet Neptune, the outermost of all the planets that wheel about the sun, had become very erratic. Ogilvy had already called attention to a suspected retardation in its velocity in December. Such a piece of news was scarcely calculated to interest a world the greater portion of whose inhabitants were unaware of the existence of the planet Neptune, nor outside the astronomical profession did the subsequent discovery of a faint remote speck of light in the region of the perturbed planet cause any very great excitement. Scientific people, however, found the intelligence remarkable enough, even before it became known that the new body was rapidly growing larger and brighter, that its motion was quite different from the orderly progress of the planets, and that the deflection of Neptune and its satellite was becoming now of an unprecedented kind.

Few people without a training in science can realise the huge isolation of the solar system. The sun with its specks of planets, its dust of planetoids, and its impalpable comets, swims in a vacant immensity that almost defeats the imagination. Beyond the orbit of Neptune there is space,

H.G. Wells was one of the early giants in the field of science fiction, and his stories are as pregnant with insight and meaning today as they were a century ago.

vacant so far as human observation has penetrated, without warmth or light or sound, blank emptiness, for twenty million times a million miles. That is the smallest estimate of the distance to be traversed before the very nearest of the stars is attained. And, saving a few comets more unsubstantial than the thinnest flame, no matter had ever to human knowledge crossed this gulf of space, until early in the twentieth century this strange wanderer appeared. A vast mass of matter it was, bulky, heavy, rushing without warning out of the black mystery of the sky into the radiance of the sun. By the second day it was clearly visible to any decent instrument, as a speck with a barely sensible diameter, in the constellation Leo near Regulus. In a little while an opera glass could attain it.

On the third day of the new year the newspaper readers of two hemispheres were made aware for the first time of the real importance of this unusual apparition in the heavens. "A Planetary Collision," one London paper headed the news, and proclaimed Duchaine's opinion that this strange new planet would probably collide with Neptune. The leader writers enlarged upon the topic. So that in most of the capitals of the world, on January 3rd, there was an expectation, however vague, of some imminent phenomenon in the sky; and as the night followed the sunset round the globe, thousands of men turned their eyes skyward to see—the old familiar stars just as they had always been.

Until it was dawn in London and Pollux setting and the stars overhead grown pale. The Winter's dawn it was, a sickly filtering accumulation of daylight, and the light of gas and candles shone yellow in the windows to show where people were astir. But the yawning policeman saw the thing, the busy crowds in the markets stopped agape, workmen going to their work betimes, milkmen, the drivers of news-carts, dissipation going home jaded and pale, homeless wanderers, sentinels on their beats, and in the country, labourers trudging afield, poachers slinking home, all over the dusky quickening country it could be seen—and out at sea by seamen watching for the day—a great white star, come suddenly into the westward sky!

Brighter it was than any star in our skies; brighter than the evening star at its brightest. It still glowed out white and large, no mere twinkling spot of light, but a small round clear shining disc, an hour after the day had come. And where science has not reached, men stared and feared, telling one another of the wars and pestilences that are foreshadowed by these fiery signs in the Heavens. Sturdy Boers, dusky Hottentots, Gold Coast Negroes, Frenchmen, Spaniards, Portuguese, stood in the warmth of the sunrise watching the setting of this strange new star.

And in a hundred observatories there had been suppressed excitement, rising almost to shouting pitch, as the two remote bodies had rushed together, and a hurrying to and fro, to gather photographic apparatus and spectroscope, and this appliance and that, to record this novel astonishing sight, the destruction of a world. For it was a world, a sister planet of our earth, far greater than our earth indeed, that had so suddenly flashed into flaming death. Neptune it was, had been struck, fairly and squarely, by the strange planet from outer space and the heat of the concussion had incontinently turned two solid globes into one vast mass of incandescence. Round the world that day, two hours before the dawn, went the pallid great white star, fading only as it sank westward and the sun mounted above it. Everywhere men marvelled at it, but of all those who saw it none could have marvelled more than those sailors, habitual watchers of the stars, who far away at sea had heard nothing of its advent and saw it now rise like a pigmy moon and climb zenithward and hang overhead and sink westward with the passing of the night.

And when next it rose over Europe everywhere were crowds of watchers on hilly slopes, on house-roofs, in open spaces, staring eastward for the rising of the great new star.

It rose with a white glow in front of it, like the glare of a white fire, and those who had seen it come into existence the night before cried out at the sight of it. "It is larger," they cried. "It is brighter!" And, indeed the moon a quarter full and sinking in the west was in its apparent size beyond comparison, but scarcely in all its breadth had it as much brightness now as the little circle of the strange new star.

"It is brighter!" cried the people clustering in the streets. But in the dim observatories the watchers held their breath and peered at one another. *"It is nearer,"* they said. *"Nearer!"*

And voice after voice repeated, "It is nearer," and the clicking telegraph took that up, and it trembled along telephone wires, and in a thousand cities grimy compositors fingered the type. "It is nearer." Men writing in offices, struck with a strange realisation, flung down their pens, men talking in a thousand places suddenly came upon a grotesque possibility in those words, "It is nearer." It hurried along awakening streets, it was shouted down the frost-stilled ways of quiet villages; men who had read these things from the throbbing tape stood in yellow-lit doorways shouting the news to the passers-by.

"It is nearer." Pretty women, flushed and glittering, heard the news told jestingly between the dances, and feigned an intelligent interest they did not feel. "Nearer! Indeed. How curious! How very, very clever people must be to find out things like that!"

Lonely tramps faring through the wintry night murmured those words to comfort themselves—looking skyward. "It has need to be nearer, for the night's as cold as charity. Don't seem much warmth from it if it *is* nearer, all the same."

"What is a new star to me?" cried the weeping woman kneeling beside her dead.

The schoolboy, rising early for his examination work, puzzled it out for himself—with the great white star, shining broad and bright through the frost-flowers of his window. "Centrifugal, centripetal," he said, with his chin on his fist.

"Stop a planet in its flight, rob it of its centrifugal force, what then? Centripetal has it, and down it falls into the sun! And this—!"

"Do *we* come in the way? I wonder—"

The light of that day went the way of its brethren, and with the later watches of the frosty darkness rose the strange star again. And it was now so bright that the waxing moon seemed but a pale yellow ghost of itself, hanging huge in the sunset. In a South African city a great man had married, and the streets were alight to welcome his return with his bride. "Even the skies have illuminated," said the flatterer. Under Capricorn, two Negro lovers, daring the wild beasts and evil spirits, for love of one another, crouched together in a cane brake where the fire-flies hovered. "That is our star," they whispered, and felt strangely comforted by the sweet brilliance of its light.

The master mathematician sat in his private room and pushed the papers from him. His calculations were already finished. In a small white phial there still remained a little of the drug that had kept him awake and active for four long nights. Each day, serene, explicit, patient as ever, he had given his lecture to his students, and then had come back at once to this momentous calculation. His face was grave, a little drawn and hectic from his drugged activity. For some time he seemed lost in thought. Then he went to the window, and the blind went up with a click. Half way up the sky, over the clustering roofs, chimneys and steeples of the city, hung the star.

He looked at it as one might look into the eyes of a brave enemy. "You may kill me," he said after a silence. "But I can hold you—and all the universe for that matter—in the grip of this little brain. I would not change. Even now."

He looked at the little phial. "There will be no need of

sleep again," he said. The next day at noon, punctual to the minute, he entered his lecture theatre, put his hat on the end of the table as his habit was, and carefully selected a large piece of chalk. It was a joke among his students that he could not lecture without that piece of chalk to fumble in his fingers, and once he had been stricken to impotence by their hiding his supply. He came and looked under his grey eyebrows at the rising tiers of young fresh faces, and spoke with his accustomed studied commonness of phrasing. "Circumstances have arisen—circumstances beyond my control," he said and paused, "which will debar me from completing the course I had designed. It would seem, gentlemen, if I may put the thing clearly and briefly, that—Man has lived in vain."

The students glanced at one another. Had they heard aright? Mad? Raised eyebrows and grinning lips there were, but one or two faces remained intent upon his calm grey-fringed face. "It will be interesting," he was saying, "to devote this morning to an exposition, so far as I can make it clear to you, of the calculations that have led me to this conclusion. Let us assume—"

He turned towards the blackboard, meditating a diagram in the way that was usual to him. "What was that about 'lived in vain'?" whispered one student to another. "Listen," said the other, nodding towards the lecturer.

And presently they began to understand.

That night the star rose later, for its proper eastward motion had carried it some way across Leo towards Virgo, and its brightness was so great that the sky became a luminous blue as it rose, and every star was hidden in its turn, save only Jupiter near the zenith, Capella, Aldebaran, Sirius and the pointers of the Bear. It was very white and beautiful. In many parts of the world that night a pallid halo encircled it about. It was perceptibly larger; in the clear refractive sky of the tropics it seemed as if it were nearly a quarter the size of the moon. The frost was still on the ground in England, but the world was as brightly lit as if it were midsummer moonlight. One could see to read quite ordinary print by that cold clear light, and in the cities the lamps burnt yellow and wan.

And everywhere the world was awake that night, and throughout Christendom a sombre murmur hung in the keen air over the country side like the belling of bees in the heather, and this murmurous tumult grew to a clangour in the cities. It was the tolling of the bells in a million belfry towers and steeples, summoning the people to sleep no more, to sin no more, but to gather in their churches and pray. And overhead, growing larger and brighter, as the earth rolled on its way and the night passed, rose the dazzling star.

And the streets and houses were alight in all the cities, the shipyards glared, and whatever roads led to high country were lit and crowded all night long. And in all the seas about the civilised lands, ships with throbbing engines, and ships with bellying sails, crowded with men and living creatures, were standing out to ocean and the north. For already the warning of the master mathematician had been telegraphed all over the world, and translated into a hundred tongues. The new planet and Neptune, locked in a fiery embrace, were whirling headlong, ever faster and faster towards the sun. Already every second this blazing mass flew a hundred miles, and every second its terrific velocity increased. As it flew now, indeed, it must pass a hundred million of miles wide of the earth and scarcely affect it. But near its destined path, as yet only slightly perturbed, spun the mighty planet Jupiter and his moons sweeping splendid round the sun. Every moment now the attraction between the fiery star and the greatest of the planets grew stronger. And the result of that attraction? Inevitably Jupiter would be deflected from its orbit into an elliptical path, and the burning star, swung by his attraction wide of its sunward rush, would "describe a curved path" and perhaps collide with, and certainly pass very close to, our earth. "Earthquakes, volcanic outbreaks, cyclones, sea waves, floods, and a steady rise in temperature to I know not what limit"—so prophesied the master mathematician.

And overhead, to carry out his words, lonely and cold and livid, blazed the star of the coming doom.

To many who stared at it that night until their eyes ached, it seemed that it was visibly approaching. And that night, too, the weather changed, and the frost that had gripped all Central Europe and France and England softened towards a thaw.

But you must not imagine because I have spoken of people praying through the night and people going aboard ships and people fleeing towards mountainous country that the whole world was already in a terror because of the star. As a matter of fact, use and wont still ruled the world, and save for the talk of idle moments and the splendour of the night, nine human beings out of ten were still busy at their common occupations. In all the cities the shops, save one here and there, opened and closed at their proper hours, the doctor and the undertaker plied their trades, the workers gathered in the factories, soldiers drilled, scholars studied, lovers sought one another, thieves lurked and fled, politicians planned their schemes. The presses of the newspapers roared through the nights, and many a priest of this church and that would not open his holy building to further what he considered a foolish panic. The newspapers insisted on the lesson of the year 1000—for then, too, people had anticipated the end. The star was no star—mere gas— a comet; and were it a star it could not possibly strike the earth. There was no precedent for such a thing. Common sense was sturdy everywhere, scornful, jesting, a little inclined to persecute the obdurate fearful. That night, at seven-fifteen by Greenwich time, the star would be at its nearest to Jupiter. Then the world would see the turn things would take. The master mathematician's grim warnings were treated by many as so much mere elaborate self-advertisement. Common sense at last, a little heated by argument, signified its unalterable convictions by going to bed. So, too, barbarism and savagery, already tired of the novelty, went about their nightly business, and save for a howling dog here and there, the beast world left the star unheeded.

And yet, when at last the watchers in the European States saw the star rise, an hour later it is true, but no larger than it had been the night before, there were still plenty awake to laugh at the master mathematician—to take the danger as if it had passed.

But hereafter the laughter ceased. The star grew—it grew with a terrible steadiness hour after hour, a little larger each hour, a little nearer the midnight zenith, and brighter and brighter, until it had turned night into a second day. Had it come straight to the earth instead of in a curved path, had it lost no velocity to Jupiter, it must have leapt the intervening gulf in a day, but as it was it took five days altogether to come by our planet. The next night it had become a third the size of the moon before it set to English eyes, and the thaw was assured. It rose over America near the size of the moon, but blinding white to look at, and *hot;* and a breath of hot wind blew now with its rising and gathering strength, and in Virginia, and Brazil, and down the St. Lawrence valley, it shone intermittently through a driving reek of thunder-clouds, flickering violet lightning, and hail unprecedented. In Manitoba was a thaw and devastating floods. And upon all the mountains of the earth the snow and ice began to melt that night, and all the rivers coming out of high country flowed thick and turbid, and soon—in their upper reaches—with swirling trees and the bodies of beasts and men. They rose steadily, steadily in the ghostly brilliance, and came trickling over their banks at last, behind the flying population of their valleys.

And along the coast of Argentina and up the South

Atlantic the tides were higher than had ever been in the memory of man, and the storms drove the waters in many cases scores of miles inland, drowning whole cities. And so great grew the heat during the night that the rising of the sun was like the coming of a shadow. The earthquakes began and grew until all down America, from the Arctic Circle to Cape Horn, hillsides were sliding, fissures were opening, and houses and walls crumbling to destruction. The whole side of Cotopaxi slipped out in one vast convulsion, and a tumult of lava poured out so high and broad and swift and liquid that in one day it reached the sea.

So the star, with the wan moon in its wake, marched across the Pacific, trailed the thunderstorms like the hem of a robe, and the growing tidal wave that toiled behind it, frothing and eager, poured over island and island and swept them clear of men. Until that wave came at last—in a blinding light and with the breath of a furnace, swift and terrible it came—a wall of water, fifty feet high, roaring hungrily, upon the long coasts of Asia, and swept inland across the plains of China. For a space the star, hotter now and larger and brighter than the sun in its strength, showed with pitiless brilliance the wide and populous country; towns and villages with their pagodas and trees, roads, wide cultivated fields, millions of sleepless people staring in helpless terror at the incandescent sky; and then, low and growing, came the murmur of the flood. And thus it was with millions of men that night—a flight nowhither, with limbs heavy with heat and breath fierce and scant, and the flood like a wall swift and white behind. And then death.

China was lit glowing white, but over Japan and Java and all the islands of Eastern Asia the great star was a ball of dull red fire because of the steam and smoke and ashes the volcanoes were spouting forth to salute its coming. Above was the lava, hot gases and ash, and below the seething floods, and the whole earth swayed and rumbled with the earthquake shocks. Soon the immemorial snows of Tibet and the Himalaya were melting and pouring down by ten million deepening converging channels upon the plains of Burmah and Hindostan. The tangled summits of the Indian jungles were aflame in a thousand places, and below the hurrying waters around the stems were dark objects that still struggled feebly and reflected the blood-red tongues of fire. And in a rudderless confusion a multitude of men and women fled down the broad river-ways to that one last hope of men—the open sea.

Larger grew the star, and larger, hotter, and brighter with a terrible swiftness now. The tropical ocean had lost its phosphorescence, and the whirling steam rose in ghostly wreaths from the black waves that plunged incessantly, speckled with storm-tossed ships.

And then came a wonder. It seemed to those who in Europe watched for the rising of the star that the world must have ceased its rotation. In a thousand open spaces of down and upland the people who had fled thither from the floods and the falling houses and sliding slopes of hill watched for that rising in vain. Hour followed hour through a terrible suspense, and the star rose not. Once again men set their eyes upon the old constellations they had counted lost to them forever. In England it was hot and clear overhead, though the ground quivered perpetually, but in the tropics, Sirius and Capella and Aldebaran showed through a veil of steam. And when at last the great star rose near ten hours late, the sun rose close upon it, and in the centre of its white heart was a disc of black.

Over Asia it was the star had begun to fall behind the movement of the sky, and then suddenly, as it hung over India, its light had been veiled. All the plain of India from the mouth of the Indus to the mouths of the Ganges was a shallow waste of shining water that night, out of which rose temples and palaces, mounds and hills, black with people. Every minaret was a clustering mass of people, who fell one by one into the turbid waters, as heat and terror overcame them. The whole land seemed a-wailing, and suddenly there swept a shadow across that furnace of despair, and a breath of cold wind, and a gathering of clouds, out of the cooling air. Men looking up, near blinded, at the star, saw that a black disc was creeping across the light. It was the moon, coming between the star and the earth. And even as men cried to God at this respite, out of the East with a strange inexplicable swiftness sprang the sun. And then star, sun and moon rushed together across the heavens.

So it was that presently, to the European watchers, star and sun rose close upon each other, drove headlong for a space and then slower, and at last came to rest, star and sun merged into one glare of flame at the zenith of the sky. The moon no longer eclipsed the star but was lost to sight in the brilliance of the sky. And though those who were still alive regarded it for the most part with that dull stupidity that hunger, fatigue, heat and despair engender, there were still men who could perceive the meaning of these signs. Star and earth had been at their nearest, had swung about one another, and the star had passed. Already it was receding, swifter and swifter, in the last stage of its headlong journey downward into the sun.

And then the clouds gathered, blotting out the vision of the sky, the thunder and lightning wove a garment round the world; all over the earth was such a downpour of rain as men had never before seen, and where the volcanoes flared red against the cloud canopy there descended torrents of mud. Everywhere the waters were pouring off the land, leaving mud-silted ruins, and the earth littered like a storm-worn beach with all that had floated, and the dead bodies of the men and brutes, its children. For days the water streamed off the land, sweeping away soil and trees and houses in the way, and piling huge dykes and scooping out Titanic gullies over the country side. Those were the days of darkness that followed the star and the heat. All through them, and for many weeks and months, the earthquakes continued.

But the star had passed, and men, hunger-driven and gathering courage only slowly, might creep back to their ruined cities, buried granaries, and sodden fields. Such few ships as had escaped the storms of that time came stunned and shattered and sounding their way cautiously through the new marks and shoals of once familiar ports. And as the storms subsided men perceived that everywhere the days were hotter than of yore, and the sun larger, and the moon, shrunk to a third of its former size, took now four-score days between its new and new.

But of the new brotherhood that grew presently among men, of the saving of laws and books and machines, of the strange change that had come over Iceland and Greenland and the shores of Baffin's Bay, so that the sailors coming there presently found them green and gracious, and could scarce believe their eyes, this story does not tell. Nor of the movement of mankind now that the earth was hotter, northward and southward towards the poles of the earth. It concerns itself only with the coming and the passing of the Star.

The Martian astronomers—for there are astronomers on Mars, although they are very different beings from men—were naturally profoundly interested by these things. They saw them from their own standpoint of course. "Considering the mass and temperature of the missile that was flung through our solar system into the sun," one wrote, "it is astonishing what a little damage the earth, which it missed so narrowly, has sustained. All the familiar continental markings and the masses of the seas remain intact, and indeed the only difference seems to be a shrinkage of the white discoloration (supposed to be frozen water) round either pole." Which only shows how small the vastest of human catastrophes may seem, at a distance of a few million miles.

The Angel of the Odd

An Extravaganza by Edgar Allen Poe

Iᴛ was a chilly November afternoon. I had just con-
summated an unusually hearty dinner, of which the dys-
peptic *truffe* formed not the least important item, and was
sitting alone in the dining room, with my feet upon the
fender, and at my elbow a small table which I had rolled up
to the fire, and upon which were some apologies for dessert, with some miscellaneous bottles of wine, spirit, and
liqueur. In the morning I had been reading Glover's "Leo-
nidas," Wilkie' s " Epigoniad," Lamartine's "Pilgrimage,"
Barlow's "Columbiad," Tuckermann's "Sicily," and Gris-
wold's "Curiosities"; I am willing to confess, therefore, that
I now felt a little stupid. I made effort to arouse myself by
aid of frequent Lafitte and, all failing, I betook myself to a
stray newspaper in despair. Having carefully perused the
column of "houses to let," and the column of "dogs lost,"
and then the two columns of "wives and apprentices run-
away," I attacked with great resolution the editorial matter, and, reading it from beginning to end without understanding a syllable, conceived the possibility of its being
Chinese, and so re-read it from the end to the beginning,
but with no more satisfactory result. I was about throwing
away, in disgust,

> This folio of four pages, happy work
> Which not even poets criticise,

> *Edgar Allen Poe was one of the originators of the
> modern short story.*

when I felt my attention somewhat aroused by the paragraph which follows:

"The avenues to death are numerous and strange. A London paper mentions the decease of a person from a singular cause. He was playing at 'puff the dart,' which is played with a long needle inserted in some worsted, and blown at a target through a tin tube. He placed the needle at the wrong end of the tube, and drawing his breath strongly to puff the dart forward with force, drew the needle into his throat. It entered the lungs, and in a few days killed him."

Upon seeing this I fell into a great rage, without exactly knowing why. "This thing," I exclaimed, "is a contemptible falsehood—a poor hoax—the lees of the invention of some pitiable penny-a-liner—of some wretched concoctor of accidents in Cocaigne. These fellows, knowing the extravagant gullibility of the age, set their wits to work in the imagination of improbable possibilities—of odd accidents, as they term them; but to a reflecting intellect (like mine," I added, in parenthesis, putting my forefinger unconsciously to the side of my nose), "to a contemplative understanding such as I myself possess, it seems evident at once that the marvelous increase of late in these 'odd accidents' is by far the oddest accident of all. For my own part, I intend to believe nothing henceforward that has anything of the 'singular' about it."

"Mein Gott, den, vat a vool you bees for dat!" replied one of the most remarkable voices I ever heard. At first I took it for a rumbling in my ears—such as man sometimes experiences when getting very drunk—but, upon second thought, I considered the sound as more nearly resembling that which proceeds from an empty barrel beaten with a big stick; and, in fact, this I should have concluded it to be, but for the articulation of the syllables and words. I am by no means naturally nervous, and the very few glasses of Lafitte which I had sipped served to embolden me a little, so that I felt nothing of trepidation, but merely uplifted my eyes with a leisurely movement, and looked carefully around the room for the intruder. I could not, however, perceive any one at all.

"Humph!" resumed the voice, as I continued my survey, "you mus pe so dronk as de pig, den, for not zee me as I zit here at your zide."

Hereupon I bethought me of looking immediately before my nose, and there, sure enough, confronting me at the table sat a personage nondescript, although not altogether indescribable. His body was a winepipe, or a rum-puncheon, or something of that character, and had a truly Falstaffian air. In its nether extremity were inserted two kegs, which seemed to answer all the purposes of legs. For arms there dangled from the upper portion of the carcass two tolerably long bottles, with the necks outward for hands. All the head that I saw the monster possessed of was one of those Hessian canteens which resemble a large snuff-box with a hole in the middle of the lid. This canteen (with a funnel on its top, like a cavalier cap slouched over the eyes) was set on edge upon the puncheon, with the hole toward myself; and through this hole, which seemed puckered up like the mouth of a very precise old maid, the creature was emitting certain rumbling and grumbling noises which he evidently intended for intelligible talk.

"I zay," said he, "you mos pe dronk as de pig, vor zit dare and zee me zit ere; and I zay, doo, you most pe pigger vool as de goose, to dispelief vat iz print in de print. 'Tiz de troof—dat it iz—eberry vord ob it."

"Who are you, pray?" said I, with much dignity, although somewhat puzzled; "how did you get here? and what is it you are talking about?"

"Az vor ow I com'd ere," replied the figure, "dat iz none of your pizzness; and as vor vat I be talking apout, I be talk apout vot I tink proper; and as vor who I be, vy dat is de very ting I com'd here for to let you zee for yourzelf."

"You are a drunken vagabond," said I, "and I shall ring

the bell and order my footman to kick you into the street."

"He! he! he!" said the fellow, "hu! hu! hu! dat you can't do."

"Can't do!" said I, "what do you mean?—can't do what?"

"Ring de pell," he replied, attempting a grin with his little villainous mouth.

Upon this I made an effort to get up, in order to put my threat into execution; but the ruffian just reached across the table very deliberately, and hitting me a tap on the forehead with the neck of one of the long bottles, knocked me back into the arm-chair from which I had half arisen. I was utterly astounded; and, for a moment, was quite at a loss what to do. In the meantime, he continued his talk.

"You zee," said he, "it iz te bess vor zit still; and now you shall know who I pe. Look at me! zee! I am te *Angel ov te Odd!*"

"And odd enough, too," I ventured to reply; "but I was always under the impression that an angel had wings."

"Te wing!" he cried, highly incensed, "vat I pe do mit te wing? Mein Gott! do you take me vor a shicken?"

"No—oh, no!" I replied, much alarmed, "you are no chicken—certainly not."

"Well, den, zit still and pehabe yourself, or I'll rap you again mid me vist. It iz te shicken ab te wing, und te owl ab te wing, und te imp ab te wing, und te headteuffel ab te wing. Te angel ab not te wing, and I am te *Angel ov te Odd.*"

"And your business with me at present is—is—"

"My pizzness!" ejaculated the thing, "vy vot a low bred puppy you mos pe vor to ask a gentleman und an angel apout his pizzness!"

This language was rather more than I could bear, even from an angel, so, plucking up courage, I seized a salt-cellar which lay within reach, and hurled it at the head of the intruder. Either he dodged, however, or my aim was inaccurate; for all I accomplished was the demolition of the crystal which protected the dial of the clock upon the mantelpiece.

As for the Angel, he evinced his sense of assault by giving me two or three hard consecutive raps upon the forehead as before. These reduced me at once to submission, and I am almost ashamed to confess that, either through pain or vexation, there came a few tears into my eyes.

"Mein Gott!" said the Angel of the Odd, apparently much softened at my distress; "mein Gott, te man is eder ferry dronck or ferry sorry. You mos not trink it so strong— you mos put de water in te wine. Here, trink dis, like a goot veller, und don't gry now—don't!"

Hereupon the Angel of the Odd replenished my goblet (which was about a third full of Port) with a colorless fluid that he poured from one of his hand bottles. I observed that these bottles had labels about their necks, and that these labels were inscribed "Kirschenwasser."

The considerate kindness of the Angel mollified me in no little measure; and, aided by the water with which he diluted my Port more than once, I at length regained sufficient temper to listen to his very extraordinary discourse. I cannot pretend to recount all that he told me, but I gleaned from what he said that he was the genius who presided over the contre temps of mankind, and whose business it was to bring about the *odd accidents* which are continually astonishing the skeptic. Once or twice, upon my venturing to express my total incredulity in respect to his pretensions, he grew very angry indeed, so that at length I considered it the wiser policy to say nothing at all, and let him have his own way. He talked on, therefore, at great length, while I merely leaned back in my chair with my eyes shut, and amused myself with munching raisins and flipping the stems about the room. But, by and bye, the Angel suddenly construed this behavior of mine into contempt. He arose in a terrible passion, slouched his funnel down over his eyes, swore a vast oath, uttered a threat of some character which I did not precisely comprehend, and finally made me a low bow and departed, wishing me, in the language of the archbishop in Gil-Blas, *"beaucoup de bonheur et un peu plus de bon sens."*

His departure afforded me relief. The very few glasses of Lafitte that I had sipped had the effect of rendering me drowsy, and I felt inclined to take a nap of some fifteen or twenty minutes, as is my custom after dinner. At six I had an appointment of consequence, which it was quite indispensable that I should keep. The policy of insurance for my dwelling house had expired the day before; and, some dispute having arisen, it was agreed that, at six, I should meet the board of directors of the company and settle the terms of a renewal. Glancing upward at the clock on the mantel-piece (for I felt too drowsy to take out my watch), I had the pleasure to find that I had still twenty-five minutes to spare. It was half past five; I could easily walk to the insurance office in five minutes; and my usual post prandian siestas had never been known to exceed five and twenty. I felt sufficiently safe, therefore, and composed myself to my slumbers forthwith.

Having completed them to my satisfaction, I again looked toward the time-piece, and was half inclined to believe in the possibility of odd accidents when I found that, instead of my ordinary fifteen or twenty minutes, I had been dozing only three; for it still wanted seven and twenty of the appointed hour. I betook myself again to my nap, and at length a second time awoke, when, to my utter amazement, it still wanted twenty-seven minutes of six. I jumped up to examine the clock, and found that it had ceased running. My watch informed me that it was half past seven; and, of course, having slept two hours, I was too late for my appointment. "It will make no difference," I said; "I can call at the office in the morning and apologize; in the meantime what can be the matter with the clock?" Upon examining it I discovered that one of the raisin-stems which I had been flipping about the room during the discourse of the Angel of the Odd had flown through the fractured crystal, and lodging, singularly enough, in the key-hole, with an end projecting outward, had thus arrested the revolution of the minute-hand.

"Ah!" said I; "I see how it is. This thing speaks for itself. A natural accident, such as *will* happen now and then!"

I gave the matter no further consideration, and at my usual hour retired to bed. Here, having placed a candle upon a reading-stand at the bed-head, and having made an attempt to peruse some pages of the "Omnipresence of the Deity," I unfortunately fell asleep in less than twenty seconds, leaving the light burning as it was.

My dreams were terrifically disturbed by visions of the Angel of the Odd. Methought he stood at the foot of the couch, drew aside the curtains, and, in the hollow, detestable tones of a rum-puncheon, menaced me with the bitterest vengeance for the contempt with which I had treated him. He concluded a long harangue by taking off his funnel-cap, inserting the tube into my gullet, and thus deluging me with an ocean of Kirschenwasser, which he poured, in a continuous flood, from one of the long-necked bottles that stood him instead of an arm. My agony was at length insufferable, and I awoke just in time to perceive that a rat had run off with the lighted candle from the stand, but not in season to prevent his making his escape with it through the hole. Very soon, a strong suffocating odor assailed my nostrils; the house, I clearly perceived, was on fire. In a few minutes the blaze broke forth with violence, and in an incredibly brief period the entire building was wrapped in flames. All egress from my chamber, except through a window, was cut off. The crowd, however, quickly procured and raised a long ladder. By means of this I was descending rapidly, and in apparent safety, when a huge hog, about whose rotund stomach, and indeed about whose whole air and physiognomy, there was something which reminded me of the Angel of the Odd,—when this hog, I say, which hitherto had been quietly slumbering in the mud, took it suddenly into his head that his left shoulder needed scratching, and could find no more convenient rubbing post than that afforded by the foot of my ladder. In an instant I was precipitated, and had the misfortune to fracture my arm.

This accident, with the loss of my insurance, and with the more serious loss of my hair, the whole of which had been singed off by the fire, predisposed me to serious impressions, so that, finally, I made up my mind to take a wife. There was a rich widow disconsolate for the loss of her seventh husband, and to her wounded spirit I offered the balm of my vows. She yielded a reluctant consent to my prayers. I knelt at her feet in gratitude and adoration. She blushed, and bowed her luxuriant tresses into close contact with those supplied me, temporarily, by Grandjean. I know not how the entanglement took place, but so it was. I arose with a shining pate, wigless; she in disdain and wrath, half buried in alien hair. Thus ended my hopes of the widow by an accident which could not have been anticipated, to be sure, but which the natural sequence of events had brought about.

Without despairing, however, I undertook the siege of a less implacable heart. The fates were again propitious for a brief period; but again a trivial incident interfered. Meeting my betrothed in an avenue thronged with the *elite* of the city, I was hastening to greet her with one of my best considered bows, when a small particle of some foreign matter lodging in the corner of my eye, rendered me, for the moment, completely blind. Before I could recover my sight, the lady of my love had disappeared—irreparably affronted at what she chose to consider my premeditated rudeness in passing her by ungreeted. While I stood bewildered at the suddenness of this accident (which might have happened, nevertheless, to any one under the sun), and while I still continued incapable of sight, I was accosted by the Angel of the Odd, who proffered me his aid with a civility which I had no reason to expect. He examined my disordered eye with much gentleness and skill, informed me that

I had a drop in it, and (whatever a "drop" was) took it out, and afforded me relief.

I now considered it time to die, (since fortune had so determined to persecute me), and accordingly made my way to the nearest river. Here, divesting myself of my clothes, (for there is no reason why we cannot die as we were born,) I threw myself headlong into the current; the sole witness of my fate being a solitary crow that had been seduced into the eating of brandy-saturated corn, and so had staggered away from his fellows. No sooner had I entered the water than this bird took it into its head to fly away with the most indispensable portion of my apparel. Postponing, therefore, for the present, my suicidal design, I just slipped my nether extremities into the sleeves of my coat, and betook myself to a pursuit of the felon with all the nimbleness which the case required and its circumstances would admit. But my evil destiny attended me still. As I ran at full speed, with my nose up in the atmosphere, and intent only upon the purloiner of my property, I suddenly perceived that my feet rested no longer upon *terra firma;* the fact is, I had thrown myself over a precipice, and should inevitably have been dashed to pieces, but for my good fortune in grasping the end of a long guide-rope, which depended from a passing balloon.

As soon as I sufficiently recovered my senses to comprehend the terrific predicament in which I stood or rather hung, I exerted all the power of my lungs to make that predicament known to the aeronaut overhead. But for a long time I exerted myself in vain. Either the fool could not, or the villain would not perceive me. Meantime the machine rapidly soared, while my strength even more rapidly failed. I was soon upon the point of resigning myself to my fate, and dropping quietly into the sea, when my spirits were suddenly revived by hearing a hollow voice from above, which seemed to be lazily humming an opera air. Looking up, I perceived the Angel of the Odd. He was leaning with his arms folded, over the rim of the car; and with a pipe in his mouth, at which he puffed leisurely, seemed to be upon excellent terms with himself and the universe. I was too much exhausted to speak, so I merely regarded him with an imploring air.

For several minutes, although he looked me full in the face, he said nothing. At length removing carefully his meerschaum from the right to the left corner of his mouth, he condescended to speak.

"Who pe you?" he asked, "und what der teuffel you pe do dare?"

To this piece of impudence, cruelty, and affectation, I could reply only by ejaculating the monosyllable "Help!"

"Elp!" echoed the ruffian—"not I. Dare iz te pottle—elp yourself, und pe tam'd!"

With these words he let fall a heavy bottle of Kirschenwasser which, dropping precisely upon the crown of my head, caused me to imagine that my brains were entirely knocked out. Impressed with this idea, I was about to relinquish my hold and give up the ghost with a good grace, when I was arrested by the cry of the Angel, who bade me hold on.

"Old on!" he said; "don't pe in te urry—don't. Will you pe take de odder pottle, or ave you pe got zober yet and come to your zenzes?"

I made haste, hereupon, to nod my head twice—once in the negative, meaning thereby that I would prefer not taking the other bottle at present—and once in the affirmative, intending thus to imply that I was sober and *had* positively come to my senses. By these means I somewhat softened the Angel.

"Und you pelief, ten," he inquired, "at te last? You pelief, ten, in te possibilty of te odd?"

I again nodded my head in assent.

"Und you ave pelief in me, te Angel of te Odd?"

I nodded again.

"Und you acknowledge tat you pe te blind dronk and te vool?"

I nodded once more.

"Put your right hand into your left hand preeches pocket, ten, in token ov your vull zubmission unto te Angel ov te Odd."

This thing, for very obvious reasons, I found it quite impossible to do. In the first place, my left arm had been broken in my fall from the ladder, and, therefore, had I let go my hold with the right hand, I must have let go altogether. In the second place, I could have no breeches until I came across the crow. I was therefore obliged, much to my regret, to shake my head in the negative—intending thus to give the Angel to understand that I found it inconvenient, just at that moment, to comply with his very reasonable demand! No sooner, however, had I ceased shaking my head than—

"Go to der teuffel, ten!" roared the Angel of the Odd.

In pronouncing these words, he drew a sharp knife across the guide-rope by which I was suspended, and as we then happened to be precisely over my own house, (which, during my peregrinations, had been handsomely rebuilt,) it so occurred that I tumbled headlong down the ample chimney and alit upon the dining-room hearth.

Upon coming to my senses, (for the fall had very thoroughly stunned me,) I found it about four o'clock in the morning. I lay outstretched where I had fallen from the balloon. My head grovelled in the ashes of an extinguished fire, while my feet reposed upon the wreck of a small table, overthrown, and amid the fragments of a miscellaneous dessert, intermingled with a newspaper, some broken glass and shattered bottles, and an empty jug of the Schiedam Kirschenwasser. Thus revenged himself the Angel of the Odd.

The Grunting of a Hog

A Pindaric ode by Charles Wesley

FREEBORN Pindaric never does refuse
      Either a lofty or a humble Muse:
Now in proud Sophoclean buskins sings
      Of heroes and of kings,
    Mighty numbers, mighty things;
      Now out of sight she flies,
      Rowing with gaudy wings
      Across the stormy skies;
        Then down again
        Herself she flings,
Without uneasiness or pain,
        To lice and dogs
        To cows and hogs,
And follows their melodious grunting o'er the plain.

      Harmonious hog, draw near!
        No bloody butcher's here,
        Thou needst not fear.
Harmonious hog, draw near, and from thy beauteous snout
    (Whilst we attend with ear,
      Like thine, pricked up devout,
To taste thy sugary voice, which here and there,
With wanton curls, vibrates around the circling air),
      Harmonious hog! warble some anthem out!

> *Charles Wesley, the brother of John Wesley, was best known as a hymnist, but he could crank out a smart Pindaric when properly inspired.*

As sweet as those which quavering monks, in days of yore,
    With us did roar,
    When they (alas
That the hard-hearted abbot such a coil should keep,
   And cheat 'em of their first, their sweetest sleep!)
   When they were ferreted up to midnight mass:
   Why should not the pigs on organs play,
     As well as they?
    Dear hog! thou king of meat!
    So near thy lord, mankind,
   The nicest taste can scarce a difference find!
   No more may I thy glorious gammons eat—
     No more
   Partake of the free farmer's Christmas store,
Black puddings which with fat would make your mouth
     run o'er—
   If I (though I should ne'er so long the sentence stay,
   And in my large ears' scale the thing ne'er so discreetly
     weigh),
    If I can find a difference in the notes
     Belched from the applauded throats
    Of rotten playhouse songsters all divine,—
If any difference I can find between their notes and thine,
    A noise they keep, with tune and out of tune,
     And round and flat,
     High, low, and this and that,
    That Algebra or thou or I might understand as soon.

Like the confounding lute's innumerable strings
    One of them sings.
Thy easier music's ten times more divine:
More like the one-stringed, deep, majestic trump-marine.
Prithee strike up, and cheer this drooping heart of mine.
   Not the sweet harp that's claimed by Jews,
Nor that which to the far more ancient Welsh belongs,
   Nor that which the wild Irish use,

Frighting even their own wolves with loud hubbubbaboos,
    Nor Indian dance with Indian songs,
        Nor yet
        (Which how should I so long forget?)
    The crown of all the rest,
        The very cream o' the jest,
    Amphion's noble lyre—the tongs;
    Nor, though poetic Jordan bite his thumbs
At the bold world, my Lord Mayor's flutes and kettledrums;
        Not all this instrumental dare
With thy soft, ravishing, vocal music ever to compare!

THE MAN OF ADAMANT

An Apologue by Nathaniel Hawthorne

Iɴ the old times of religious gloom and intolerance, lived Richard Digby, the gloomiest and most intolerant of a stern brotherhood. His plan of salvation was so narrow, that, like a plank in a tempestuous sea, it could avail no sinner but himself, who bestrode it triumphantly, and hurled anathemas against the wretches whom he saw struggling with the billows of eternal death. In his view of the matter, it was a most abominable crime—as, indeed, it is a great folly—for men to trust to their own strength, or even to grapple to any other fragment of the wreck, save this narrow plank, which, moreover, he took special care to keep out of their reach. In other words, as his creed was like no man's else, and being well pleased that Providence had intrusted him alone, of mortals, with the treasure of a true faith, Richard Digby determined to seclude himself to the sole and constant enjoyment of his happy fortune.

"And verily," thought he, "I deem it a chief condition of Heaven's mercy to myself, that I hold no communion with those abominable myriads which it hath cast off to perish. Peradventure, were I to tarry longer in the tents of Kedar, the gracious boon would be revoked, and I also be swallowed up in the deluge of wrath, or consumed in the storm of fire and brimstone, or involved in whatever new kind of ruin is ordained for the horrible perversity of this generation."

So Richard Digby took an axe, to hew space enough for a tabernacle in the wilderness, and some few other necessaries, especially a sword and gun, to smite and slay any

> *Nathaniel Hawthorne wrote superb short stories, carved from the rock of his native New England.*

intruder upon his hallowed seclusion; and plunged into the dreariest depths of the forest. On its verge, however, he paused a moment, to shake off the dust of his feet against the village where he had dwelt, and to invoke a curse on the meeting-house, which he regarded as a temple of heathen idolatry. He felt a curiosity, also, to see whether the fire and brimstone would not rush down from Heaven at once, now that the one righteous man had provided for his own safety. But, as the sunshine continued to fall peacefully on the cottages and fields, and the husbandmen labored and children played, and as there were many tokens of present happiness, and nothing ominous of a speedy judgment, he turned away, somewhat disappointed. The further he went, however, and the lonelier he felt himself, and the thicker the trees stood along his path, and the darker the shadow overhead, so much the more did Richard Digby exult. He talked to himself, as he strode onward; he read his Bible to himself, as he sat beneath the trees; and, as the gloom of the forest hid the blessed sky, I had almost added, that, at morning, noon, and eventide, he prayed to himself. So congenial was this mode of life to his disposition, that he often laughed to himself, but was displeased when an echo tossed him back the long, loud roar.

In this manner, he journeyed onward three days and two nights, and came, on the third evening, to the mouth of a cave, which, at first sight, reminded him of Elijah's cave at Horeb, though perhaps it more resembled Abraham's sepulchral cave, at Machpelah. It entered into the heart of a rocky hill. There was so dense a veil of tangled foliage about it, that none but a sworn lover of gloomy recesses would have discovered the low arch of its entrance, or have dared to step within its vaulted chamber, where the burning eyes of a panther might encounter him. If Nature meant this remote and dismal cavern for the use of man, it could only be to bury in its gloom the victims of a pestilence, and then to block up its mouth with stones, and avoid the spot forever after. There was nothing bright nor cheerful near it, except a bubbling fountain, some twenty paces off, at which Richard Digby hardly threw away a glance. But he thrust his head into the cave, shivered, and congratulated himself.

"The finger of Providence hath pointed my way!" cried he, aloud, while the tomb-like den returned a strange echo, as if some one within were mocking him. "Here my soul will be at peace; for the wicked will not find me. Here I can read the Scriptures and be no more provoked with lying interpretations. Here I can offer up acceptable prayers because my voice will not be mingled with the sinful supplications of the multitude. Of a truth, the only way to heaven leadeth through the narrow entrance of this cave,— and I alone have found it!"

In regard to this cave, it was observable that the roof, so far as the imperfect light permitted it to be seen, was hung with substances resembling opaque icicles; for the damps of unknown centuries, dripping down continually, had become as hard as adamant; and wherever that moisture fell, it seemed to possess the power of converting what it bathed to stone. The fallen leaves and sprigs of foliage, which the wind had swept into the cave, and the little feathery shrubs, rooted near the threshold, were not wet with a natural dew, but had been embalmed by this wondrous process. And here I am put in mind that Richard Digby, before he withdrew himself from the world, was supposed by skilful physicians to have contracted a disease for which no remedy was written in their medical books. It was a deposition of calculous particles within his heart, caused by an obstructed circulation of the blood; and, unless a miracle should be wrought for him, there was danger that the malady might act on the entire substance of the organ, and change his fleshy heart to stone. Many, indeed, affirmed that the process was already near its consummation. Richard Digby, however, could never be convinced that any such direful work was going on within him; nor when he saw the sprigs of marble foliage, did his heart even throb the quicker, at the similitude suggested by these once tender herbs. It may be that this same insensibility was a symptom of the disease.

Be that as it might, Richard Digby was well contented with his sepulchral cave. So dearly did he love this congenial spot, that, instead of going a few paces to the bubbling spring for water, he allayed his thirst with now and then a drop of moisture from the roof, which, had it fallen anywhere but on his tongue, would have been congealed into a pebble. For a man predisposed to stoniness of the heart, this surely was unwholesome liquor. But there he dwelt, for three days more, eating herbs and roots, drinking his own destruction, sleeping, as it were, in a tomb, and awaking to the solitude of death, yet esteeming this horrible mode of life as hardly inferior to celestial bliss. Perhaps superior; for, above the sky, there would be angels to disturb him. At the close of the third day he sat in the portal of his mansion, reading the Bible aloud, because no other ear could profit by it, and reading it amiss, because the rays of the setting sun did not penetrate the dismal depth of shadow round about him, nor fall upon the sacred page. Suddenly, however, a faint gleam of light was thrown over the volume, and, raising his eyes, Richard Digby saw that a young woman stood before the mouth of the cave, and that the sunbeams bathed her white garment, which thus seemed to possess a radiance of its own.

"Good-evening, Richard," said the girl; "I have come from afar to find thee."

The slender grace and gentle loveliness of this young woman were at once recognized by Richard Digby. Her name was Mary Goffe. She had been a convert to his preaching of the word in England, before he yielded himself to that exclusive bigotry which now enfolded him with such an iron grasp that no other sentiment could reach his bosom. When he came a pilgrim to America, she had remained in her father's hall; but now, as it appeared, had crossed the ocean after him, impelled by the same faith that led other exiles hither, and perhaps by love almost as holy. What else but faith and love united could have sustained so delicate a creature, wandering thus far into the forest, with her golden hair dishevelled by the boughs, and her feet wounded by the thorns? Yet, weary and faint though she must have been, and affrighted at the dreariness of the cave, she looked on the lonely man with a mild and pitying expression, such as might beam from an angel's eyes, towards an afflicted mortal. But the recluse, frowning sternly upon her, and keeping his finger between the leaves of his half-closed Bible, motioned her away with his hand.

"Off!" cried he. "I am sanctified, and thou art sinful. Away!"

"O, Richard," said she, earnestly, "I have come this weary way because I heard that a grievous distemper had seized upon thy heart; and a great Physician hath given me the skill to cure it. There is no other remedy than this which I have brought thee. Turn me not away, therefore, nor refuse my medicine; for then must this dismal cave be thy sepulchre."

"Away!" replied Richard Digby, still with a dark frown. "My heart is in better condition than thine own. Leave me, earthly one; for the sun is almost set; and when no light reaches the door of the cave, then is my prayer-time."

Now, great as was her need, Mary Goffe did not plead with this stony-hearted man for shelter and protection, nor ask anything whatever for her own sake. All her zeal was for his welfare.

"Come back with me!" she exclaimed, clasping her hands,—"come back to thy fellow-men; for they need thee, Richard, and thou hast ten-fold need of them. Stay not in this evil den; for the air is chill, and the damps are fatal; nor will any that perish within it ever find the path to heaven. Hasten hence, I entreat thee, for thine own soul's sake; for either the roof will fall upon thy head, or some other speedy destruction is at hand."

"Perverse woman!" answered Richard Digby, laughing aloud,—for he was moved to bitter mirth by her foolish vehemence,—"I tell thee that the path to heaven leadeth straight through this narrow portal where I sit. And, moreover, the destruction thou speakest of is ordained, not for this blessed cave, but for all other habitations of mankind, throughout the earth. Get thee hence speedily, that thou mayst have thy share!"

So saying, he opened his Bible again, and fixed his eyes intently on the page, being resolved to withdraw his thoughts from this child of sin and wrath, and to waste no more of his holy breath upon her. The shadow had now grown so deep, where he was sitting, that he made continual mistakes in what he read, converting all that was gracious and merciful to denunciations of vengeance and unutterable woe on every created being but himself. Mary Goffe, meanwhile, was leaning against a tree, beside the sepulchral cave, very sad, yet with something heavenly and ethereal in her unselfish sorrow. The light from the setting sun still glorified her form and was reflected a little way within the darksome den, discovering so terrible a gloom that the maiden shuddered for its self-doomed inhabitant. Espying the bright fountain near at hand, she hastened thither, and scooped up a portion of its water in a cup of birchen bark. A few tears mingled with the draught, and perhaps gave it all its efficacy. She then returned to the mouth of the cave, and knelt down at Richard Digby's feet.

"Richard," she said, with passionate fervor, yet a gentleness in all her passion, "I pray thee, by thy hope of heaven, and as thou wouldst not dwell in this tomb forever, drink of this hallowed water, be it but a single drop! Then, make room for me by thy side, and let us read together one page of that blessed volume,—and, lastly, kneel down with me and pray! Do this, and thy stony heart shall become softer than a babe's, and all be well."

But Richard Digby, in utter abhorrence of the proposal, cast the Bible at his feet, and eyed her with such a fixed and evil frown, that he looked less like a living man than a marble statue, wrought by some dark-imagined sculptor to express the most repulsive mood that human features could assume. And, as his look grew even devilish, so, with an equal change, did Mary Goffe become more sad, more mild, more pitiful, more like a sorrowing angel. But, the more heavenly she was, the more hateful did she seem to Richard Digby, who at length raised his hand, and smote down the cup of hallowed water upon the threshold of the cave, thus rejecting the only medicine that could have cured his stony heart. A sweet perfume lingered in the air for a moment, and then was gone.

"Tempt me no more, accursed woman," exclaimed he, still with his marble frown, "lest I smite thee down also! What hast thou to do with my prayers?—what with my heaven?"

No sooner had he spoken these dreadful words, than Richard Digby's heart ceased to beat; while—so the legend says—the form of Mary Goffe melted into the last sunbeams, and returned from the sepulchral cave to heaven. For Mary Goffe had been buried in an English church-yard, months before; and either it was her ghost that haunted the wild forest, or else a dreamlike spirit, typifying pure Religion.

Above a century afterwards, when the trackless forest of Richard Digby's day had long been interspersed with settlements, the children of a neighboring farmer were playing at the foot of a hill. The trees, on account of the rude and broken surface of this acclivity, had never been felled, and were crowded so densely together as to hide all but a few rocky prominences, wherever their roots could grapple with the soil. A little boy and girl, to conceal themselves from their playmates, had crept into the deepest shade, where not only the darksome pines, but a thick veil of creeping plants suspended from an overhanging rock, combined to make a twilight at noonday, and almost a midnight at all other seasons. There the children hid themselves, and shouted, repeating the cry at intervals, till the whole party of pursuers were drawn thither, and pulling aside the matted foliage, let in a doubtful glimpse of daylight. But scarcely was this accomplished, when the little group uttered a simultaneous shriek, and tumbled headlong down the hill, making the best of their way homeward, without a second glance into the gloomy recess. Their father, unable to comprehend what had so startled them, took his axe, and, by felling one or two trees, and tearing away the creeping plants, laid the mystery open to the day. He had discovered the entrance of a cave, closely resembling the mouth of a sepulchre, within which sat the figure of a man, whose gesture and attitude warned the father and children to stand back, while his visage wore a most forbidding frown. This repulsive personage seemed to have been carved in the same gray stone that formed the walls and portal of the cave. On minuter inspection, indeed, such blemishes were observed, as made it doubtful whether the figure were really a statue, chiselled by human art, and somewhat worn and defaced by the lapse of ages, or a freak of Nature, who might have chosen to imitate, in stone, her usual handiwork of flesh. Perhaps it was the least unreasonable idea, suggested by this strange spectacle, that the moisture of the cave possessed a petrifying quality, which had thus awfully embalmed a human corpse.

There was something so frightful in the aspect of this Man of Adamant, that the farmer, the moment that he recovered from the fascination of his first gaze, began to heap stones into the mouth of the cavern. His wife, who had followed him to the hill, assisted her husband's efforts. The children, also, approached as near as they durst, with their little hands full of pebbles, and cast them on the pile. Earth was then thrown into the crevices, and the whole fabric overlaid with sods. Thus all traces of the discovery were obliterated, leaving only a marvellous legend, which grew wilder from one generation to another, as the children told it to their grandchildren, and they to their posterity, till few believed that there had ever been a cavern or a statue, where now they saw but a grassy path on the shadowy hill-side. Yet, grown people avoid the spot, nor do children play there. Friendship, and Love, and Piety, all human and celestial sympathies, should keep aloof from that hidden cave; for there still sits, and, unless an earthquake crumble down the roof upon his head, shall sit forever, the shape of Richard Digby, in the attitude of repelling the whole race of mortals—not from heaven—but from the horrible loneliness of his dark, cold sepulchre!

THE AMERICAN'S TALE

A Story by Sir Arthur Conan Doyle

"**I**T air strange, it air," he was saying as I opened the door of the room where our social little semi-literary society met; "but I could tell you queerer things than that 'ere—almighty queer things. You can't learn everything out of books, sirs, nohow. You see it ain't the men as can string English together and as has had good eddications as finds themselves in the queer places I've been in. They're mostly rough men, sirs, as can scarce speak aright, far less tell with pen-and-ink the things they've seen; but if they could they'd make some of your European's har riz with astonishment. They would, sirs, you bet!"

His name was Jefferson Adams, I believe; I know his initials were J. A., for you may see them yet deeply whittled on the right-hand upper panel of our smoking-room door. He left us this legacy, and also some artistic patterns done in tobacco juice upon our Turkey carpet; but beyond these reminiscences our American storyteller has vanished from our ken. He gleamed across our ordinary quiet conviviality like some brilliant meteor, and then was lost in the outer darkness. That night, however, our Nevada friend was in full swing; and I quietly lit my pipe and dropped into the nearest chair, anxious not to interrupt his story.

"Mind you," he continued, "I hain't got no grudge against your men of science. I likes and respects a chap as can match every beast and plant, from a huckleberry to a grizzly with a jaw-breakin' name; but if you wants real

> *Sir Arthur Conan Doyle authored many wonderful stories that never even mentioned Sherlock Holmes.*

interestin' facts, something a bit juicy, you go to your whalers and your frontiersmen, and your scouts and Hudson Bay men, chaps who mostly can scarce sign their names."

There was a pause here, as Mr. Jefferson Adams produced a long cheroot and lit it. We preserved a strict silence in the room, for we had already learned that on the slightest interruption our Yankee drew himself into his shell again. He glanced round with a self-satisfied smile as he remarked our expectant looks, and continued through a halo of smoke,

"Now which of you gentlemen has ever been in Arizona? None, I'll warrant. And of all English or Americans as can put pen to paper, how many has been in Arizona? Precious few, I calc'late. I've been there, sirs, lived there for years; and when I think of what I've seen there, why, I can scarce get myself to believe it now.

"Ah, there's a country! I was one of Walker's filibusters, as they chose to call us; and after we'd busted up, and the chief was shot, some of us made tracks and located down there. A reg'lar English and American colony, we was, with our wives and children, and all complete. I reckon there's some of the old folk there yet, and that they hain't forgotten what I'm agoing to tell you. No, I warrant they hain't, never on this side of the grave, sirs.

"I was talking about the country, though; and I guess I could astonish you considerable if I spoke of nothing else. To think of such a land being built for a few 'Greasers' and half-breeds! It's a misusing of the gifts of Providence, that's what I calls it. Grass as hung over a chap's head as he rode through it, and trees so thick that you couldn't catch a glimpse of blue sky for leagues and leagues, and orchids like umbrellas! Maybe some of you has seen a plant as they calls the 'fly-catcher,' in some parts of the States?"

"Dionæa muscipula," murmured Dawson, our scientific man *par excellence*.

"Ah, 'Die near a municipal,' that's him! You'll see a fly

stand on that 'ere plant, and then you'll see the two sides of a leaf snap up together and catch it between them, and grind it up and mash it to bits, for all the world like some great sea squid with its beak; and hours after, if you open the leaf, you'll see the body lying half-digested, and in bits. Well, I've seen those flytraps in Arizona with leaves eight and ten feet long, and thorns or teeth a foot or more; why, they could—But darn it, I'm going too fast!

"It's about the death of Joe Hawkins I was going to tell you; 'bout as queer a thing, I reckon, as ever you heard tell on. There wasn't nobody in Montana as didn't know of Joe Hawkins—'Alabama' Joe, as he was called there. A reg'lar out and outer, he was, 'bout the darndest skunk as ever man clapt eyes on. He was a good chap enough, mind ye, as long as you stroked him the right way; but rile him anyhow, and he were worse nor a wild-cat. I've seen him empty his six-shooter into a crowd as chanced to jostle him agoing into Simpson's bar when there was a dance on; and he bowied Tom Hooper 'cause he spilt his liquor over his weskit by mistake. No, he didn't stick at murder, Joe didn't; and he weren't a man to be trusted further nor you could see him.

"Now at the time I tell on, when Joe Hawkins was swaggerin' about the town and layin' down the law with his shootin'-irons, there was an Englishman there of the name of Scott—Tom Scott, if I rec'lects aright. This chap Scott was a thorough Britisher (beggin' the present company's pardon), and yet he didn't freeze much to the British set there, or they didn't freeze much to him. He was a quiet simple man, Scott was—rather too quiet for a rough set like that; sneakin' they called him, but he weren't that. He kept hisself mostly apart, an' didn't interfere with nobody so long as he were left alone. Some said as how he'd been kinder ill-treated at home—been a Chartist, or something of that sort, and had to up stick and run; but he never spoke of it hisself, an' never complained. Bad luck or good, that chap kept a stiff lip on him.

"This chap Scott was a sort o' butt among the men about Montana, for he was so quiet an' simple-like. There was no party either to take up his grievances; for, as I've been saying, the Britishers hardly counted him one of them, and many a rough joke they played on him. He never cut up rough, but was polite to all hisself. I think the boys got to think he hadn't much grit in him till he showed 'em their mistake.

"It was in Simpson's bar as the row got up, an' that led to the queer thing I was going to tell you of. Alabama Joe and one or two other rowdies were dead on the Britishers in those days, and they spoke their opinions pretty free, though I warned them as there'd be an almighty muss. That partic'lar night Joe was nigh half drunk, an' he swaggered about the town with his sixshooter, lookin' out for a quarrel. Then he turned into the bar where he know'd he'd find some o' the English as ready for one as he was hisself. Sure enough, there was half a dozen lounging about, an' Tom Scott standin' alone before the stove. Joe sat down by the table, and put his revolver and bowie down in front of him. 'Them's my arguments, Jeff,' he says to me, 'if any white-livered Britisher dares give me the lie.' I tried to stop him, sirs; but he weren't a man as you could easily turn, an' he began to speak in a way as no chap could stand. Why, even a 'Greaser' would flare up if you said as much of Greaserland! There was a commotion at the bar, an' every man laid his hands on his wepin's; but afore they could draw we heard a quiet voice from the stove: 'Say your prayers, Joe Hawkins; for, by Heaven, you're a dead man!' Joe turned, round and looked like grabbin' at his iron; but it weren't no manner of use. Tom Scott was standing up, covering him with his Derringer; a smile on his white face, but the very devil shining in his eye. 'It ain't that the old country has used me over-well,' he says, 'but no man shall speak agin it afore me, and live.' For a second or two I could see his finger tighten round the trigger, an' then he gave a laugh, an' threw the pistol on the floor. 'No,' he says, 'I can't shoot a half-drunk man. Take your dirty life, Joe, an' use it better nor you have done. You've been nearer the grave this night than you will be agin until your time comes. You'd best make tracks now, I guess. Nay, never look black at me, man; I'm not afeard at your shootin'-iron. A bully's nigh always a coward.' And he swung contemptuously round, and relit his half-smoked pipe from the stove; while Alabama slunk out o' the bar, with the laughs of the Britishers ringing in his ears. I saw his face as he passed me, and on it I saw murder, sirs—murder, as plain as ever I seed anything in my life.

"I stayed in the bar after the row, and watched Tom Scott as he shook hands with the men about. It seemed kinder queer to me to see him smilin' and cheerful-like; for I knew Joe's bloodthirsty mind, and that the Englishman had small chance of ever seeing the morning. He lived in an out-of-the-way sort of place, you see, clean off the trail, and had to pass through the Flytrap Gulch to get to it. This here gulch was a marshy gloomy place, lonely enough during the day even; for it were always a creepy sort o' thing to see the great eight- and ten-foot leaves snapping up if aught touched them; but at night there were never a soul near. Some parts of the marsh, too, were soft and deep, and a body thrown in would be gone by the morning. I could see Alabama Joe crouchin' under the leaves of the great Flytrap in the darkest part of the gulch, with a scowl on his face and a revolver in his hand; I could see it, sirs, as plain as with my two eyes.

" 'Bout midnight Simpson shuts up his bar, so out we had to go. Tom Scott started off for his three-mile walk at a slashing pace. I just dropped him a hint as he passed me, for I kinder liked the chap. 'Keep your Derringer loose in your belt, sir,' I says, 'for you might chance to need it.' He looked round at me with his quiet smile, and then I lost sight of him in the gloom. I never thought to see him again.

He'd hardly gone afore Simpson comes up to me and says, 'There'll be a nice job in the Flytrap Gulch to-night, Jeff; the boys say that Hawkins started half an hour ago to wait for Scott and shoot him on sight. I calc'late the coroner'll be wanted to-morrow.'

"What passed in the gulch that night? It were a question as were asked pretty free next morning. A half-breed was in Ferguson's store after daybreak, and he said as he'd chanced to be near the gulch 'bout one in the morning. It warn't easy to get at his story, he seemed so uncommon scared; but he told us, at last, as he'd heard the fearfulest screams in the stillness of the night. There weren't no shots, he said, but scream after scream, kinder muffled, like a man with a serape over his head, an' in mortal pain. Abner Brandon and me, and a few more, was in the store at the time; so we mounted and rode out to Scott's house, passing through the gulch on the way. There weren't nothing partic'lar to be seen there—no blood nor marks of a fight, nor nothing; and when we gets up to Scott's house, out he comes to meet us as fresh as a lark. 'Hullo, Jeff!' says he, 'no need for the pistols after all. Come in an' have a cocktail, boys.' 'Did ye see or hear nothing as ye came home last night?' says I. 'No,' says he; 'all was quiet enough. An owl kinder moaning in the Flytrap Gulch—that was all. Come, jump off and have a glass.' 'Thank ye,' said Abner. So off we gets, and Tom Scott rode into the settlement with us when we went back.

"An all-fired commotion was on in Main street as we rode into it. The 'Merican party seemed to have gone clean crazed. Alabama Joe was gone, not a darned particle of him left. Since he went out to the gulch nary eye had seen him. As we got off our horses there was a considerable crowd in front of Simpson's, and some ugly looks at Tom Scott, I can tell you. There was a clickin' of pistols, and I saw as Scott had his hand in his bosom too. There weren't a single English face about. 'Stand aside, Jeff Adams,' says Zebb

Humphrey, as great a scoundrel as ever lived, 'you hain't got no hand in this game. Say, boys, are we, free Americans, to be murdered by any darned Britisher?' It was the quickest thing as ever I seed. There was a rush an' a crack; Zebb was down, with Scott's ball in his thigh, and Scott hisself was on the ground with a dozen men holding him. It weren't no use struggling, so he lay quiet. They seemed a bit uncertain what to do with him at first, but then one of Alabama's special chums put them up to it. 'Joe's gone,' he said; 'nothing ain't surer nor that, an' there lies the man as killed him. Some of you knows as Joe went on business to the gulch last night; he never came back. That 'ere Britisher passed through after he'd gone; they'd had a row, screams is heard 'mong the great flytraps. I say agin he has played poor Joe some o' his sneakin' tricks, an' thrown him into the swamp. It ain't no wonder as the body is gone. But air we to stan' by and see English murderin' our own chums? I guess not. Let Judge Lynch try him, that's what I say.' 'Lynch him!' shouted a hundred angry voices—for all the rag-tag an' bobtail o' the settlement was round us by this time. 'Here, boys, fetch a rope, and swing him up. Up with him over Simpson's door!' 'See here though,' says another, coming forrards; 'let's hang him by the great flytrap in the gulch. Let Joe see as he's revenged, if so be as he's buried 'bout theer.' There was a shout for this, an' away they went, with Scott tied on his mustang in the middle, and a mounted guard, with cocked revolvers, round him; for we knew as there was a score or so Britishers about, as didn't seem to recognise Judge Lynch, and was dead on a free fight.

"I went out with them, my heart bleedin' for Scott, though he didn't seem a cent put out, he didn't. He were game to the backbone. Seems kinder queer, sirs, hangin' a man to a flytrap; but our'n were a reg'lar tree, and the leaves like a brace of boats with a hinge between 'em and thorns at the bottom.

"We passed down the gulch to the place where the great

one grows, and there we seed it with the leaves, some open, some shut. But we seed something worse nor that. Standin' round the tree was some thirty men, Britishers all, an' armed to the teeth. They was waitin' for us evidently, an' had a businesslike look about 'em, as if they'd come for something and meant to have it. There was the raw material there for about as warm a scrimmidge as ever I seed. As we rode up, a great redbearded Scotchman—Cameron were his name—stood out afore the rest, his revolver cocked in his hand. 'See here, boys,' he says, 'you've got no call to hurt a hair of that man's head. You hain't proved as Joe is dead yet; and if you had, you hain't proved as Scott killed him. Anyhow, it were in self-defence; for you all know as he was lying in wait for Scott, to shoot him on sight; so I say agin, you hain't got no call to hurt that man; and what's more, I've got thirty six-barrelled arguments against your doin' it.' 'It's an interestin' pint, and worth arguin' out,' said the man as was Alabama Joe's special chum. There was a clickin' of pistols, and a loosenin' of knives, and the two parties began to draw up to one another, an' it looked like a rise in the mortality of Montana. Scott was standing behind with a pistol at his ear if he stirred, lookin' quiet and composed as having no money on the table, when sudden he gives a start an' a shout as rang in our ears like a trumpet. 'Joe!' he cried, 'Joe! Look at him! In the flytrap!' We all turned an' looked where he was pointin'. Jerusalem! I think we won't get that picter out of our minds agin. One of the great leaves of the flytrap, that had been shut and touchin' the ground as it lay, was slowly rolling back upon its hinges. There, lying like a child in its cradle, was Alabama Joe in the hollow of the leaf. The great thorns had been slowly driven through his heart as it shut upon him. We could see as he'd tried to cut his way out, for there was a slit in the thick fleshy leaf, an' his bowie was in his hand; but it had smothered him first. He'd lain down on it likely to keep the damp off while he were awaitin' for Scott, and it had closed on him as you've seen your little hothouse ones do on a fly; an' there he were as we found him, torn and crushed into pulp by the great jagged teeth of the man-eatin' plant. There, sirs, I think you'll own as that's a curious story."

"And what became of Scott?" asked Jack Sinclair.

"Why, we carried him back on our shoulders, we did, to Simpson's bar, and he stood us liquors round. Made a speech too—a darned fine speech—from the counter. Somethin' about the British lion an' the 'Merican eagle walkin' arm in arm for ever an' a day. And now, sirs, that yarn was long, and my cheroot's out, so I reckon I'll make tracks afore it's later"; and with a "Good-night!" he left the room.

"A most extraordinary narrative!" said Dawson. "Who would have thought a Dionæa had such power!"

"Deuced rum yarn!" said young Sinclair.

"Evidently a matter-of-fact truthful man," said the doctor.

"Or the most original liar that ever lived," said I.

I wonder which he was.

THE FURNISHED ROOM

A story by O. Henry

RESTLESS, shifting, fugacious as time itself is a certain vast bulk of the population of the red brick district of the lower West Side. Homeless, they have a hundred homes. They flit from furnished room to furnished room, transients forever—transients in abode, transients in heart and mind. They sing "Home, Sweet Home" in ragtime; they carry their *lares et penates* in a bandbox; their vine is entwined about a picture hat; a rubber plant is their fig tree.

Hence the houses of this district, having had a thousand dwellers, should have a thousand tales to tell, mostly dull ones, no doubt; but it would be strange if there could not be found a ghost or two in the wake of all these vagrant guests.

One evening after dark a young man prowled among these crumbling red mansions, ringing their bells. At the twelfth he rested his lean handbaggage upon the step and wiped the dust from his hatband and forehead. The bell sounded faint and far away in some remote, hollow depths.

To the door of this, the twelfth house whose bell he had rung, came a housekeeper who made him think of an unwholesome, surfeited worm that had eaten its nut to a hollow shell and now sought to fill the vacancy with edible lodgers.

He asked if there was a room to let.

"Come in," said the housekeeper. Her voice came from

O. Henry is known for the ironic endings to his short stories, etched from his penetrating insight into the conflicts that rage deep within the human heart.

her throat; her throat seemed lined with fur. "I have the third-floor back, vacant since a week back. Should you wish to look at it?"

The young man followed her up the stairs. A faint light from no particular source mitigated the shadows of the halls. They trod noiselessly upon a stair carpet that its own loom would have forsworn. It seemed to have become vegetable; to have degenerated in that rank, sunless air to lush lichen or spreading moss that grew in patches to the staircase and was viscid under the foot like organic matter. At each turn of the stairs were vacant niches in the wall. Perhaps plants had once been set within them. If so they had died in that foul and tainted air. It may be that statues of the saints had stood there, but it was not difficult to conceive that imps and devils had dragged them forth in the darkness and down to the unholy depths of some furnished pit below.

"This is the room," said the housekeeper, from her furry throat. "It's a nice room. It ain't often vacant. I had some most elegant people in it last summer—no trouble at all, and paid in advance to the minute. The water's at the end of the hall. Sprowls and Mooney kept it three months. They done a vaudeville sketch. Miss B'retta Sprowls—you may have heard of her—Oh, that was just the stage names— right there over the dresser is where the marriage certificate hung, framed. The gas is here, and you see there is plenty of closet room. It's a room everybody likes. It never stays idle long."

"Do you have many theatrical people rooming here?" asked the young man.

"They comes and goes. A good proportion of my lodgers is connected with the theatres. Yes, sir, this is the theatrical district. Actor people never stays long anywhere. I get my share. Yes, they comes and they goes."

He engaged the room, paying for a week in advance. He was tired, he said, and would take possession at once.

He counted out the money. The room had been made ready, she said, even to towels and water. As the housekeeper moved away he put, for the thousandth time, the question that he carried at the end of his tongue.

"A young girl—Miss Vashner—Miss Eloise Vashner—do you remember such a one among your lodgers? She would be singing on the stage, most likely. A fair girl, of medium height and slender, with reddish, gold hair and dark mole near her left eyebrow."

"No, I don't remember the name. Them stage people has names they change as often as their rooms. They comes and they goes. No, I don't call that one to mind."

No. Always no. Five months of ceaseless interrogation and the inevitable negative. So much time spent by day in questioning managers, agents, schools and choruses; by night among the audiences of theatres from all-star casts down to music halls so low that he dreaded to find what he most hoped for. He who had loved her best had tried to find her. He was sure that since her disappearance from home this great, water-girt city held her somewhere, but it was like a monstrous quicksand, shifting its particles constantly, with no foundation, its upper granules of today buried to-morrow in ooze and slime.

The furnished room received its latest guest with a first glow of pseudo-hospitality, a hectic, haggard, perfunctory welcome like the specious smile of a demirep. The sophistical comfort came in reflected gleams from the decayed furniture, the ragged brocade upholstery of a couch and two chairs, a foot-wide cheap pier glass between the two windows, from one or two gilt picture frames and a brass bedstead in a corner.

The guest reclined, inert, upon a chair, while the room, confused in speech as though it were an apartment in Babel, tried to discourse to him of its divers tenantry.

A polychromatic rug like some brilliant-flowered, rectangular, tropical islet lay surrounded by a billowy sea of soiled matting. Upon the gay-papered wall were those pictures that pursue the homeless one from house to house—The Huguenot Lovers, The First Quarrel, The Wedding Breakfast, Psyche at the Fountain. The mantel's chastely severe outline was ingloriously veiled behind some pert drapery drawn rakishly askew like the sashes of the Amazonian ballet. Upon it was some desolate flotsam cast aside by the room's marooned when a lucky sail had borne them to a fresh port—a trifling vase or two, pictures of actresses, a medicine bottle, some stray cards out of a deck.

One by one, as the characters of a cryptograph became explicit, the little signs left by the furnished rooms' procession of guests developed a significance. The threadbare space in the rug in front of the dresser told that lovely woman had marched in the throng. The tiny fingerprints on the wall spoke of little prisoners trying to feel their way to sun and air. A splattered stain, raying like the shadow of a bursting bomb, witnessed where a hurled glass or bottle had splintered with its contents against the wall. Across the pier glass had been scrawled with a diamond in staggering letters the name "Marie." It seemed that the succession of dwellers in the furnished room had turned in fury—perhaps tempted beyond forbearance by its garish coldness—and wreaked upon it their passions. The furniture was chipped and bruised; the couch, distorted by bursting springs, seemed a horrible monster that had been slain during the stress of some grotesque convulsion. Some more potent upheaval had cloven a great slice from the marble mantel. Each plank in the floor owned its particular cant and shriek as from a separate and individual agony. It seemed incredible that all this malice and injury had been wrought upon the room by those who had called it for a time their home; and yet it may have been the cheated home instinct surviving blindly, the resentful rage at false household gods that had kindled their wrath. A hut that is our own we can sweep and adorn and cherish.

The young tenant in the chair allowed these thoughts to file, softshod, through his mind, while there drifted into the room furnished sounds and furnished scents. He heard in one room a tittering and incontinent, slack laughter; in others the monologue of a scold, the rattling of dice, a lullaby, and one crying dully; above him a banjo tinkled with spirit. Doors banged somewhere; the elevated trains roared intermittently; a cat yowled miserably upon a back fence. And he breathed the breath of the house—a dank savor rather than a smell—a cold, musty effluvium as from underground vaults mingled with the reeking exhalations of linoleum and mildewed and rotten woodwork.

Then suddenly, as he rested there, the room was filled with the strong, sweet odor of mignonette. It came as upon a single buffet of wind with such sureness and fragrance and emphasis that it almost seemed a living visitant. And the man cried aloud: "What, dear?" as if he had been called, and sprang up and faced about. The rich odor clung to him and wrapped him around. He reached out his arms for it, all his senses for the time confused and commingled. How could one be peremptorily called by an odor? Surely it must have been a sound. But, was it not the sound that had touched, that had caressed him?

"She has been in this room," he cried, and he sprang to wrest from it a token, for he knew he would recognize the smallest thing that had belonged to her or that she had touched. This enveloping scent of mignonette, the odor that she had loved and made her own—whence came it?

The room had been but carelessly set in order. Scattered upon the flimsy dresser scarf were half a dozen hairpins—those discreet, indistinguishable friends of womankind, feminine of gender, infinite of mood and uncommunicative of tense. These he ignored, conscious of their triumphant lack of identity. Ransacking the drawers of the dresser he came upon a discarded, tiny, ragged handkerchief. He pressed it to his face. It was racy and insolent with heliotrope; he hurled it to the floor. In another drawer he found odd buttons, a theatre programme, a pawnbroker's card, two lost marshmallows, a book on the divination of dreams. In the last was a woman's black satin hair bow, which halted him, poised between ice and fire. But the black satin hair bow also is femininity's demure, impersonal common ornament and tells no tales.

And then he traversed the room like a hound on the scent, skimming the walls, considering the corners of the bulging matting on his hands and knees, rummaging mantel and tables, the curtains and hangings, the drunken cabinet in the corner, for a visible sign, unable to perceive that she was there beside, around, against, within, above him, clinging to him, wooing him, calling him so poignantly through the finer senses that even his grosser ones became cognizant of the call. Once again he answered loudly: "Yes, dear!" and turned, wild-eyed, to gaze on vacancy, for he could not yet discern form and color and love and outstretched arms in the odor of mignonette. Oh, God! whence that odor, and since when have odors had a voice to call? Thus he groped.

He burrowed in crevices and corners, and found corks and cigarettes. These he passed in passive contempt. But once he found in a fold of the matting a half-smoked cigar, and this he ground beneath his heel with a green and trenchant oath. He sifted the room from end to end. He found dreary and ignoble small records of many a peripatetic tenant; but of her whom he sought, and who may have lodged there, and whose spirit seemed to hover there, he found no trace.

And then he thought of the housekeeper.

He ran from the haunted room downstairs and to a door that showed a crack of light. She came out to his knock. He smothered his excitement as best he could.

"Will you tell me, madam," he besought her, "who occupied the room I have before I came?"

"Yes, sir. I can tell you again. 'Twas Sprowls and

Mooney, as I said. Miss B'retta Sprowls it was in the theatres, but Missis Mooney she was. My house is well known for respectability. The marriage certificate hung framed, on a nail over—"

"What kind of a lady was Miss Sprowls—in looks, I mean?"

"Why, black-haired, sir, short, and stout, with a comical face. They left a week ago Tuesday."

"And before they occupied it?"

"Why, there was a single gentleman connected with the draying business. He left owing me a week. Before him was Missis Crowder and her two children, that stayed four months; and back of them was old Mr. Doyle, whose sons paid for him. He kept the room six months. That goes back a year, sir, and further I do not remember."

He thanked her and crept back to his room. The room was dead. The essence that had vivified it was gone. The perfume of mignonette had departed. In its place was the old, stale odor of mouldy house furniture, of atmosphere in storage.

The ebbing of his hope drained his faith. He sat staring at the yellow, singing gaslight. Soon he walked to the bed and began to tear the sheets into strips. With the blade of his knife he drove them tightly into every crevice around windows and door. When all was snug and taut he turned out the light, turned the gas full on again and laid himself gratefully upon the bed.

It was Mrs. McCool's night to go with the can for beer. So she fetched it and sat with Mrs. Purdy in one of those subterranean retreats where housekeepers foregather and the worm dieth seldom.

"I rented out my third-floor-back this evening," said Mrs. Purdy, across a fine circle of foam. "A young man took it. He went up to bed two hours ago."

"Now, did ye, Mrs. Purdy, ma'am?" said Mrs. McCool,

with intense admiration. "You do be a wonder for rentin' rooms of that kind. And did ye tell him, then?" she concluded in a husky whisper laden with mystery.

"Rooms," said Mrs. Purdy, in her furriest tones, "are furnished for to rent. I did not tell him, Mrs. McCool."

" 'Tis right ye are, ma'am; 'tis by renting rooms we kape alive. Ye have the rale sense for business, ma'am. There be many people will rayjict the rentin' of a room if they be tould a suicide has been after dyin' in the bed of it."

"As you say, we has our living to be making," remarked Mrs. Purdy.

"Yis, ma'am; 'tis true. 'Tis just one wake ago this day I helped ye lay out the third-floor-back. A pretty slip of a colleen she was to be killin' herself wid the gas—a swate little face she had, Mrs. Purdy, ma'am."

"She'd a-been called handsome, as you say," said Mrs. Purdy, assenting but critical, "but for that mole she had a-growin' by her left eyebrow. Do fill up your glass again, Mrs. McCool."

THE MIRACLE OF PURUN BHAGAT

A Story by Rudyard Kipling

The night we felt the earth would move
  We stole and plucked him by the hand,
Because we loved him with the love
  That knows but cannot understand.

And when the roaring hillside broke,
  And all our world fell down in rain,
We saved him, we the Little Folk;
  But lo! he does not come again.

Mourn now, we saved him for the sake
  Of such poor love as wild ones may,
Mourn ye! Our brother will not wake,
  And his own kind drive us away!
            —*Dirge of the Langurs*

T<small>HERE</small> was once a man in India who was Prime Minister of one of the semi-independent native States in the northwestern part of the country. He was a Brahmin, so high-caste that caste ceased to have any particular meaning for him; and his father had been an important official in the gay-colored tag-rag and bobtail of an old-fashioned

> *Rudyard Kipling brought both adventure and the Indian subcontinent alive in his many stories and poems.*

Hindu Court. But as Purun Dass grew up he felt that the old order of things was changing, and that if any one wished to get on in the world he must stand well with the English, and imitate all that the English believed to be good. At the same time a native official must keep his own master's favor. This was a difficult game, but the quiet, close-mouthed young Brahmin, helped by a good English education at a Bombay University, played it coolly, and rose, step by step, to be Prime Minister of the kingdom. That is to say, he held more real power than his master, the Maharajah.

When the old king—who was suspicious of the English, their railways and telegraphs—died, Purun Dass stood high with his young successor, who had been tutored by an Englishman; and between them, though he always took care that his master should have the credit, they established schools for little girls, made roads, and started State dispensaries and shows of agricultural implements, and published a yearly blue-book on the "Moral and Material Progress of the State," and the Foreign Office and the Government of India were delighted. Very few native States take up English progress altogether, for they will not believe, as Purun Dass showed he did, that what was good for the Englishman must be twice as good for the Asiatic. The Prime Minister became the honored friend of Viceroys and Governors, and Lieutenant-Governors, and medical missionaries, and common missionaries, and hard-riding English officers who came to shoot in the State preserves, as well as of whole hosts of tourists who traveled up and down India in the cold weather, showing how things ought to be managed. In his spare time he would endow scholarships for the study of medicine and manufactures on strictly English lines, and write letters to the "Pioneer," the greatest Indian daily paper, explaining his master's aims and objects.

At last he went to England on a visit, and had to pay

enormous sums to the priests when he came back; for even so high-caste a Brahmin as Purun Dass lost caste by crossing the black sea. In London he met and talked with every one worth knowing—men whose names go all over the world—and saw a great deal more than he said. He was given honorary degrees by learned universities, and he made speeches and talked of Hindu social reform to English ladies in evening dress, till all London cried, "This is the most fascinating man we have ever met at dinner since cloths were first laid."

When he returned to India there was a blaze of glory, for the Viceroy himself made a special visit to confer upon the Maharajah the Grand Cross of the Star of India—all diamonds and ribbons and enamel; and at the same ceremony, while the cannon boomed, Purun Dass was made a Knight Commander of the Order of the Indian Empire; so that his name stood Sir Purun Dass, K.C.I.E.

That evening, at dinner in the big Viceregal tent, he stood up with the badge and the collar of the Order on his breast, and replying to the toast of his master's health, made a speech few Englishmen could have bettered.

Next month, when the city had returned to its sun-baked quiet, he did a thing no Englishman would have dreamed of doing; for, so far as the world's affairs went, he died. The jeweled order of his knighthood went back to the Indian Government, and a new Prime Minister was appointed to the charge of affairs, and a great game of General Post began in all the subordinate appointments. The priests knew what had happened and the people guessed; but India is the one place in the world where a man can do as he pleases and nobody asks why; and the fact that Dewan Sir Purun Dass, K.C.I.E., had resigned position, palace, and power, and taken up the begging-bowl and ocher-colored dress of a Sunnyasi or holy man, was considered nothing extraordinary. He had been, as the Old Law recommends, twenty years a youth, twenty years a fighter,—though he had never carried a weapon in his life,—and twenty years head of a household. He had used his wealth and his power for what he knew both to be worth; he had taken honor when it came his way; he had seen men and cities far and near, and men and cities had stood up and honored him. Now he would let these things go, as a man drops the cloak he no longer needs.

Behind him, as he walked through the city gates, an antelope skin and brass-handled crutch under his arm, and a begging-bowl of polished brown *coco-de-mer* in his hand, barefoot, alone, with eyes cast on the ground—behind him they were firing salutes from the bastions in honor of his happy successor. Purun Dass nodded. All that life was ended; and he bore it no more ill-will or good-will than a man bears to a colorless dream of the night. He was a Sunnyasi—a houseless wandering mendicant, depending on his neighbors for his daily bread; and so long as there is a morsel to divide in India neither priest nor beggar starves. He had never in his life tasted meat, and very seldom eaten even fish. A five-pound note would have covered his personal expenses for food through any one of the many years in which he had been absolute master of millions of money. Even when he was being lionized in London he had held before him his dream of peace and quiet—the long, white, dusty Indian road, printed all over with bare feet, the incessant, slow-moving traffic, and the sharp-smelling wood smoke curling up under the fig-trees in the twilight, where the wayfarers sit at their evening meal.

When the time came to make that dream true the Prime Minister took the proper steps, and in three days you might more easily have found a bubble in the trough of the long Atlantic seas than Purun Dass among the roving, gathering, separating millions of India.

At night his antelope skin was spread where the darkness overtook him—sometimes in a Sunnyasi monastery by the roadside; sometimes by a mud pillar shrine of Kala

Pir, where the Jogis, who are another misty division of holy men, would receive him as they do those who know what castes and divisions are worth; sometimes on the outskirts of a little Hindu village, where the children would steal up with the food their parents had prepared; and sometimes on the pitch of the bare grazing-grounds, where the flame of his stick fire waked the drowsy camels. It was all one to Purun Dass—or Purun Bhagat, as he called himself now. Earth, people, and food were all one. But unconsciously his feet drew him away northward and eastward; from the south to Rohtak; from Rohtak to Kurnool; from Kurnool to ruined Samanah, and then up-stream along the dried bed of the Gugger river that fills only when the rain falls in the hills, till one day he saw the far line of the great Himalayas.

Then Purun Bhagat smiled, for he remembered that his mother was of Rajput Brahmin birth; from Kulu way— a Hill-woman, always homesick for the snows—and that the least touch of Hill blood draws a man at the end back to where he belongs.

"Yonder," said Purun Bhagat, breasting the lower slopes of the Sewaliks, where the cacti stand up like seven-branched candlesticks—"yonder I shall sit down and get knowledge"; and the cool wind of the Himalayas whistled about his ears as he trod the road that led to Simla.

The last time he had come that way it had been in state, with a clattering cavalry escort, to visit the gentlest and most affable of Viceroys; and the two had talked for an hour together about mutual friends in London, and what the In-dian common folks really thought of things. This time Purun Bhagat paid no calls, but leaned on the rail of the Mall, watching that glorious view of the Plains spread out forty miles below, till a native Mohammedan policeman told him he was obstructing traffic; and Purun Bhagat salaamed reverently to the Law, because he knew the value of it, and was seeking for a Law of his own. Then he moved on, and slept that night in an empty hut at Chota Simla, last end of the earth, but it was only the beginning of his journey. He followed the Himalaya-Thibet road, the little ten-foot track that is blasted out of solid rock, or strutted out on timbers over gulfs a thousand feet deep; that dips into warm, wet, shut-in valleys, and climbs out across bare, grassy hill-shoulders where the sun strikes like a burning-glass; or turns through dripping, dark forests where the tree-ferns dress the trunks from head to heel, and the pheasant calls to his mate. And he met Thibetan herdsmen with their dogs and flocks of sheep, each sheep with a little bag of borax on his back, and wandering woodcutters, and cloaked and blanketed Lamas from Thibet, coming into India on pilgrimage, and envoys of little solitary Hill-states, posting furiously on ring-streaked and piebald ponies, or the cavalcade of a Rajah paying a visit; or else for a long, clear day he would see nothing more than a black bear grunting and rooting below in the valley. When he first started, the roar of the world he had left still rang in his ears, as the roar of a tunnel rings long after the train has passed through; but when he had put the Mutteeanee Pass behind him that was all done, and Purun Bhagat was alone with himself, walking, wondering, and thinking, his eyes on the ground, and his thoughts with the clouds.

One evening he crossed the highest pass he had met till then—it had been a two days' climb—and came out on a line of snow-peaks that banded all the horizon—mountains from fifteen to twenty thousand feet high, looking almost near enough to hit with a stone, though they were fifty or sixty miles away. The pass was crowned with dense, dark forest—deodar, walnut, wild cherry, wild olive, and wild pear, but mostly deodar, which is the Himalayan cedar; and under the shadow of the deodars stood a deserted shrine to Kali—who is Durga, who is Sitala, who is sometimes worshiped against the smallpox.

Purun Dass swept the stone floor clean, smiled at the grinning statue, made himself a little mud fireplace at the back of the shrine, spread his antelope skin on a bed of fresh pine-needles, tucked his *bairagi*—his brass-handled crutch—under his armpit, and sat down to rest.

Immediately below him the hillside fell away, clean and cleared for fifteen hundred feet, where a little village of stone-walled houses, with roofs of beaten earth, clung to the steep tilt. All round it the tiny terraced fields lay out like aprons of patchwork on the knees of the mountain, and cows no bigger than beetles grazed between the smooth stone circles of the threshing-floors. Looking across the valley, the eye was deceived by the size of things, and could not at first realize that what seemed to be low scrub, on the opposite mountain-flank, was in truth a forest of hundred-foot pines. Purun Bhagat saw an eagle swoop across the gigantic hollow, but the great bird dwindled to a dot ere it was half-way over. A few bands of scattered clouds strung up and down the valley, catching on a shoulder of the hills, or rising up and dying out when they were level with the head of the pass. And "Here shall I find peace," said Purun Bhagat.

Now, a Hill-man makes nothing of a few hundred feet up or down, and as soon as the villagers saw the smoke in the deserted shrine, the village priest climbed up the terraced hillside to welcome the stranger.

When he met Purun Bhagat's eyes—the eyes of a man used to control thousands—he bowed to the earth, took the begging-bowl without a word, and returned to the village, saying, "We have at last a holy man. Never have I seen such a man. He is of the Plains—but pale-colored—a Brahmin of the Brahmins." Then all the housewives of the village said, "Think you he will stay with us?" and each did her best to cook the most savory meal for the Bhagat. Hill-food is very simple, but with buckwheat and Indian corn, and rice and red pepper, and little fish out of the stream in the valley, and honey from the flue-like hives built in the stone walls, and dried apricots, and turmeric, and wild ginger, and bannocks of flour, a devout woman can make good things, and it was a full bowl that the priest carried to the Bhagat. Was he going to stay? asked the priest. Would he need a *chela*—a disciple—to beg for him? Had he a blanket against the cold weather? Was the food good?

Purun Bhagat ate, and thanked the giver. It was in his mind to stay. That was sufficient, said the priest. Let the begging-bowl be placed outside the shrine, in the hollow made by those two twisted roots, and daily should the Bhagat be fed; for the village felt honored that such a man— he looked timidly into the Bhagat's face—should tarry among them.

That day saw the end of Purun Bhagat's wanderings. He had come to the place appointed for him—the silence and the space. After this, time stopped, and he, sitting at the mouth of the shrine, could not tell whether he were alive or dead; a man with control of his limbs, or a part of the hills, and the clouds, and the shifting rain and sunlight. He would repeat a Name softly to himself a hundred hundred times, till, at each repetition, he seemed to move more and more out of his body, sweeping up to the doors of some tremendous discovery; but, just as the door was opening, his body would drag him back, and, with grief, he felt he was locked up again in the flesh and bones of Purun Bhagat.

Every morning the filled begging-bowl was laid silently in the crutch of the roots outside the shrine. Sometimes the priest brought it; sometimes a Ladakhi trader, lodging in the village, and anxious to get merit, trudged up the path; but, more often, it was the woman who had cooked the meal overnight; and she would murmur, hardly above her breath: "Speak for me before the gods, Bhagat. Speak for such a one, the wife of so-and-so !" Now and then some bold child would be allowed the honor, and Purun Bhagat would hear him drop the bowl and run as fast as his little legs could carry him, but the Bhagat never came down to the village. It was laid out like a map at his feet. He could see the evening gatherings, held on the circle of the threshing-floors because that was the only level ground; could see the wonderful unnamed green of the young rice, the indigo blues of the Indian corn, the dock-like patches of buckwheat, and, in its season, the red bloom of the amaranth, whose tiny seeds, being neither grain nor pulse, make a food that can be lawfully eaten by Hindus in time of fasts.

When the year turned, the roofs of the huts were all little squares of purest gold, for it was on the roofs that they laid out their cobs of the corn to dry. Hiving and harvest, rice sowing and husking, passed before his eyes, all embroidered down there on the many-sided plots of fields, and he thought of them all, and wondered what they all led to at the long last.

Even in populated India a man cannot a day sit still before the wild things run over him as though he were a rock; and in that wilderness very soon the wild things, who knew Kali's Shrine well, came back to look at the intruder. The *langurs,* the big gray-whiskered monkeys of the Himalayas, were, naturally, the first, for they are alive with curiosity; and when they had upset the begging bowl, and rolled it round the floor, and tried their teeth on the brass-handled crutch, and made faces at the antelope skin, they decided that the human being who sat so still was harmless. At evening, they would leap down from the pines, and beg with their hands for things to eat, and then swing off in graceful curves. They liked the warmth of the fire, too, and huddled round it till Purun Bhagat had to push them aside to throw on more fuel; and in the morning, as often as not, he would find a furry ape sharing his blanket. All day long, one or other of the tribe would sit by his side, staring out at the snows, crooning and looking unspeakably wise and sorrowful.

After the monkeys came the *barasingh,* that big deer which is like our red deer, but stronger. He wished to rub off the velvet of his horns against the cold stones of Kali's statue, and stamped his feet when he saw the man at the shrine. But Purun Bhagat never moved, and, little by little, the royal stag edged up and nuzzled his shoulder. Purun Bhagat slid one cool hand along the hot antlers, and the touch soothed the fretted beast, who bowed his head, and Purun very softly rubbed and raveled off the velvet. Afterward, the *barasingh* brought his doe and fawn—gentle things that mumbled on the holy man's blanket—or would come alone at night; his eyes green in the fire-flicker to take his share of fresh walnuts. At last, the musk-deer, the shyest and almost the smallest of the deerlets, came, too, her big rabbity ears erect; even brindled, silent *mushick-nabha* must needs find out what the light in the shrine meant, and drop her moose-like nose into Purun Bhagat's lap, coming and going with the shadows of the fire. Purun Bhagat called them all "my brothers," and his low call of *"Bhai ! Bhai!"* would draw them from the forest at noon if they were within earshot. The Himalayan black bear, moody and suspicious— Sona, who has the V-shaped white mark under his chin— passed that way more than once; and since the Bhagat showed no fear, Sona showed no anger, but watched him, and came closer; and begged a share of the caresses, and a dole of bread or wild berries. Often, in the still dawns, when the Bhagat would climb to the very crest of the pass to watch the red day walking along the peaks of the snows, he would find Sona shuffling and grunting at his heels, thrusting a curious fore-paw under fallen trunks, and bringing it away with a *whoof* of impatience; or his early steps would wake Sona where he lay curled up, and the great brute, rising erect, would think to fight, till he heard the Bhagat's voice and knew his best friend.

Nearly all hermits and holy men who live apart from the big cities have the reputation of being able to work miracles with the wild things, but all the miracle lies in keeping still, in never making a hasty movement, and, for a long time, at least, in never looking directly at a visitor. The villagers saw the outline of the *barasingh* stalking like a shadow through the dark forest behind the shrine; saw the *minaul,* the Himalayan pheasant, blazing in her best colors before Kali's statue, and the *langurs* on their haunches, inside playing with the walnut shells. Some of the children; too, had heard Sona singing to himself, bear-fashion, behind the fallen rocks, and the Bhagat's reputation as miracle-worker stood firm.

Yet nothing was further from his mind than miracles. He believed that all things were one big miracle, and when a man knows that much he knows something to go upon. He knew for a certainty that there was nothing great and nothing little in this world; and day and night he strove to think out his way into the heart of things, back to the place whence his soul had come.

So thinking, his untrimmed hair fell down about his shoulders, the stone slab at the side of the antelope skin was dented into a little hole by the foot of his brass-handled crutch, and the place between the tree-trunks, where the begging-bowl rested day after day, sunk and wore into a hollow almost as smooth as the brown shell itself; and each beast knew his exact place at the fire. The fields changed their colors with the seasons; the threshing-floors filled and emptied, and filled again and again; and again and again, when winter came, the *langurs* frisked among the branches feathered with light snow, till the mother monkeys brought their sad-eyed little babies up from the warmer valleys with the spring. There were few changes in the village. The priest was older, and many of the little children who used to come with the begging-dish sent their own children now; and when you asked of the villagers how long their holy man had lived in Kali's Shrine at the head of the pass, they answered, "Always."

Then came such summer rains as had not been known in the Hills for many seasons. Through three good months the valley was wrapped in cloud and soaking mist—steady, unrelenting downfall, breaking off into thunder-shower after thunder-shower. Kali's Shrine stood above the clouds, for the most part, and there was a whole month in which the Bhagat never saw his village. It was packed away under a white floor of cloud that swayed and shifted and rolled on itself and bulged upward, but never broke from its piers—the streaming flanks of the valley.

All that time he heard nothing but the sound of a million little waters, overhead from the trees, and underfoot along the ground, soaking through the pine-needles, dripping from the tongues of draggled fern, and spouting in newly torn muddy channels down the slopes. Then the sun came out, and drew forth the good incense of the deodars and the rhododendrons, and that far-off clean smell which the Hill people call "the smell of the snows." The hot sunshine lasted for a week, and then the rains gathered together for their last downpour, and the water fell in sheets that flayed off the skin of the ground and leaped back in mud. Purun Bhagat heaped his fire high that night, for he was sure his brothers would need warmth; but never a beast came to the shrine, though he called and called till he dropped asleep, wondering what had happened in the woods.

It was in the black heart of the night, the rain drumming like a thousand drums, that he was roused by a plucking at his blanket, and, stretching out, felt the little hand of a *langur.* "It is better here than in the trees," he said sleepily, loosening a fold of blanket; "take it and be warm." The monkey caught his hand and pulled hard. "Is it food, then?" said Purun Bhagat. "Wait awhile, and I will prepare some." As he kneeled to throw fuel on the fire the *langur* ran to the door of the shrine, crooned, and ran back again, plucking at the man's knee.

"What is it? What is thy trouble, Brother?" said Purun Bhagat, for the *langur's* eyes were full of things that he could not tell. "Unless one of thy caste be in a trap—and none set traps here—I will not go into that weather. Look, Brother, even the *barasingh* comes for shelter!"

The deer's antlers clashed as he strode into the shrine, clashed against the grinning statue of Kali. He lowered them in Purun Bhagat's direction and stamped uneasily, hissing through his half-shut nostrils.

"Hai! Hai! Hai!" said the Bhagat, snapping his fingers. "Is *this* payment for a night's lodging?" But the deer pushed him toward the door, and as he did so Purun Bhagat heard the sound of something opening with a sigh, and saw two slabs of the floor draw away from each other, while the sticky earth below smacked its lips.

"Now I see," said Purun Bhagat. "No blame to my brothers that they did not sit by the fire to-night. The mountain is falling. And yet—why should I go?" His eye fell on the empty begging-bowl, and his face changed. "They have given me good food daily since—since I came, and, if I am not swift, to-morrow there will not be one mouth in the valley. Indeed, I must go and warn them below. Back there, Brother! Let me get to the fire."

The *barasingh* backed unwillingly as Purun Bhagat drove a pine torch deep into the flame, twirling it till it was well lit. "Ah! ye came to warn me," he said, rising. "Better than that we shall do; better than that. Out, now, and lend me thy neck, Brother, for I have but two feet."

He clutched the bristling withers of the *barasingh* with his right hand, held the torch away with his left, and stepped out of the shrine into the desperate night. There was no breath of wind, but the rain nearly drowned the flare as the great deer hurried down the slope, sliding on his haunches. As soon as they were clear of the forest more of the Bhagat's brothers joined them. He heard, though he could not see, the *langurs* pressing about him, and behind them the *uhh! uhh!* of Sona. The rain matted his long white hair into ropes; the water splashed beneath his bare feet, and his yellow robe clung to his frail old body, but he stepped down steadily, leaning against the *barasingh*. He was no longer a holy man, but Sir Purun Dass, K.C.I.E., Prime Minister of no small State, a man accustomed to command, going out to save life. Down the steep, plashy path they poured all together, the Bhagat and his brothers, down and down till the deer's feet clicked and stumbled on the wall of a threshing-floor, and he snorted because he smelt Man. Now they were at the head of the one crooked village street, and the Bhagat beat with his crutch on the barred windows of the blacksmith's house as his torch blazed up in the shelter of the eaves. "Up and out !" cried Purun Bhagat; and he did not know his own voice, for it was years since he had spoken aloud to a man. "The hill falls! The hill is falling! Up and out, oh, you within!"

"It is our Bhagat," said the blacksmith's wife. "He stands among his beasts. Gather the little ones and give the call."

It ran from house to house, while the beasts, cramped in the narrow way, surged and huddled round the Bhagat, and Sona puffed impatiently.

The people hurried into the street—they were no more than seventy souls all told—and in the glare of the torches they saw their Bhagat holding back the terrified *barasingh*, while the monkeys plucked piteously at his skirts, and Sona sat on his haunches and roared.

"Across the valley and up the next hill!" shouted Purun Bhagat. "Leave none behind! We follow!"

Then the people ran as only Hill folk can run, for they knew that in a landslip you must climb for the highest ground across the valley. They fled, splashing through the little river at the bottom, and panted up the terraced fields on the far side, while the Bhagat and his brethren followed. Up and up the opposite mountain they climbed; calling to each other by name—the roll-call of the village—and at their heels toiled the big *barasingh*, weighted by the failing strength of Purun Bhagat. At last the deer stopped in the shadow of a deep pine-wood, five hundred feet up the hillside. His instinct, that had warned him of the coming slide, told him he would be safe here.

Purun Bhagat dropped fainting by his side, for the chill of the rain and that fierce climb were killing him; but first he called to the scattered torches ahead, "Stay and count your numbers; then, whispering to the deer as he saw the lights gather in a cluster: "Stay with me, Brother. Stay—till—I—go!"

There was a sigh in the air that grew to a mutter, and a mutter that grew to a roar, and a roar that passed all sense of hearing, and the hillside on which the villagers stood was hit in the darkness, and rocked to the blow. Then a note as steady, deep, and true as the deep C of the organ drowned everything for perhaps five minutes, while the very roots of the pines quivered to it. It died away, and the sound of the rain falling on miles of hard ground and grass changed to the muffled drum of water on soft earth. That told its own tale.

Never a villager—not even the priest—was bold enough to speak to the Bhagat who had saved their lives. They crouched under the pines and waited till the day. When it came they looked across the valley and saw that what had been forest, and terraced field, and track threaded grazing-ground was one raw, red, fan-shaped smear, with a few trees flung head-down on the scarp. That red ran high up the hill of their refuge, damming back the little river, which had begun to spread into a brick-colored lake. Of the village, of the road to the shrine, of the shrine itself, and the forest behind, there was not trace. For one mile in width and two thousand feet in sheer depth the mountain-side had come away bodily, planed clean from head to heel.

And the villagers, one by one, crept through the wood to pray before their Bhagat. They saw the *barasingh* standing over him, who fled when they came near, and they heard the *langurs* wailing in the branches, and Sona moaning up the hill; but their Bhagat was dead, sitting cross-legged, his back against a tree, his crutch under his armpit, and his face turned to the northeast.

The priest said: "Behold a miracle after a miracle, for in this very attitude must all Sunnyasis be buried! Therefore where he now is we will build the temple to our holy man."

They built the temple before a year was ended—a little stone-and-earth shrine—and they called the hill the Bhagat's Hill, and they worship there with lights and flowers and offerings to this day. But they do not know that the saint of their worship is the late Sir Purun Dass, K.C.I.E., D.C.L., Ph.D., etc., once Prime Minister of the progressive and enlightened State of Mohiniwala, and honorary or corresponding member of more learned and scientific societies than will ever do any good in this world or the next.

Why I Became A Business Man

A memoir by Andrew Carnegie

WHY did I become a business man? I am sure that I should never have selected a business career if I had been permitted to choose.

The eldest son of parents who were themselves poor, I had, fortunately, to begin to perform some useful work in the world while still very young in order to earn an honest livelihood, and was thus shown even in early boyhood that my duty was to assist my parents and, like them, become, as soon as possible, a bread-winner in the family. What I could get to do, not what I desired, was the question.

When I was born my father was a well-to-do master weaver in Dunfermline, Scotland. He owned no less than four damask-looms and employed apprentices. This was before the days of steam-factories for the manufacture of linen. A few large merchants took orders, and employed master weavers, such as my father, to weave the cloth, the merchants supplying the materials.

As the factory system developed hand-loom weaving naturally declined, and my father was one of the sufferers by the change. The first serious lesson of my life came to me one day when he had taken in the last of his work to the merchant, and returned to our little home greatly distressed because there was no more work for him to do. I was

> *Andrew Carnegie became the richest man in the world—then spent the last years of his life giving away his fortune for the good of mankind. Hundreds of libraries throughout the world are Carnegie libraries.*

then just about ten years of age, but the lesson burned into my heart, and I resolved then that the wolf of poverty should be driven from our door some day, if I could do it.

The question of selling the old looms and starting for the United States came up in the family council, and I heard it discussed from day to day. It was finally resolved to take the plunge and join relatives already in Pittsburgh. I well remember that neither father nor mother thought the change would be otherwise than a great sacrifice for them, but that "it would be better for the two boys."

In after life, if you can look back as I do and wonder at the complete surrender of their own desires which parents make for the good of their children, you must reverence their memories with feelings akin to worship.

On arriving in Allegheny City (there were four of us: father, mother, my younger brother, and myself), my father entered a cotton factory. I soon followed, and served as a "bobbin-boy," and this is how I began my preparation for subsequent apprenticeship as a business man. I received one dollar and twenty cents a week, and was then just about twelve years old.

I cannot tell you how proud I was when I received my first week's own earnings. One dollar and twenty cents made by myself and given to me because I had been of some use in the world! No longer entirely dependent upon my parents, but at last admitted to the family partnership as a contributing member and able to help them! I think this makes a man out of a boy sooner than almost anything else, and a real man, too, if there be any germ of true manhood in him. It is everything to feel that you are useful.

I have had to deal with great sums. Many millions of dollars have since passed through my hands. But the genuine satisfaction I had from that one dollar and twenty cents outweighs any subsequent pleasure in money getting. It was the direct reward of honest, manual labor; it represented a week of very hard work—so hard that, but for the aim and end which sanctified it, slavery might not be much too strong a term to describe it.

For a lad of twelve to rise and breakfast every morning, except the blessed Sunday morning, and go into the streets and find his way to the factory and begin to work while it was still dark outside, and not be released until after darkness came again in the evening, forty minutes' interval only being allowed at noon, was a terrible task.

But I was young and had my dreams, and something within always told me that this would not, could not, should not last—I should some day get into a better position. Besides this, I felt myself no longer a mere boy, but quite a little man, and this made me happy.

A change soon came, for a kind old Scotsman, who knew some of our relatives, made bobbins, and took me into his factory before I was thirteen. But here for a time it was even worse than in the cotton factory, because I was set to fire a boiler in the cellar, and actually to run the small steam engine which drove the machinery. The firing of the boiler was all right, for fortunately we did not use coal, but the refuse wooden chips; and I always liked to work in wood. But the responsibility of keeping the water right and of running the engine, and the danger of my making a mistake and blowing the whole factory to pieces, caused too great a strain, and I often awoke and found myself sitting up in bed through the night, trying the steam gauges. But I never told them at home that I was having a hard tussle. No, no! everything must be bright to them.

This was a point of honor, for every member of the family was working hard, except, of course, my little brother, who was then a child, and we were telling each other only all the bright things. Besides this, no man would whine and give up—he would die first.

There was no servant in our family, and several dollars per week were earned by the mother by binding shoes after her daily work was done! Father was also hard at work in the factory. And could I complain?

My kind employer, John Hay—peace to his ashes!—soon relieved me of the undue strain, for he needed some one to make out bills and keep his accounts, and finding that I could write a plain schoolboy hand and could "cipher," he made me his only clerk. But still I had to work hard upstairs in the factory, for the clerking took but little time.

You know how people moan about poverty as being a great evil, and it seems to be accepted that if people had only plenty of money and were rich, they would be happy and more useful, and get more out of life.

As a rule, there is more genuine satisfaction, a truer life, and more obtained from life in the humble cottages of the poor than in the palaces of the rich. I always pity the sons and daughters of rich men, who are attended by servants, and have governesses at a later age, but am glad to remember that they do not know what they have missed.

They have kind fathers and mothers, too, and think that they enjoy the sweetness of these blessings to the fullest: but this they cannot do; for the poor boy who has in his father his constant companion, tutor, and model, and in his mother—holy name!—his nurse, teacher, guardian angel, saint, all in one, has a richer, more precious fortune in life than any rich man's son who is not so favored can possibly know, and compared with which all other fortunes count for little.

It is because I know how sweet and happy and pure the home of honest poverty is, how free from perplexing care, from social envies and emulations, how loving and how united its members may be in the common interest of supporting the family, that I sympathize with the rich man's boy and congratulate the poor man's boy; and it is for these reasons that from the ranks of the poor so many strong, eminent, self-reliant men have always sprung and always must spring.

If you will read the list of the immortals who "were not born to die," you will find that most of them have been born to the precious heritage of poverty.

It seems, nowadays, a matter of universal desire that poverty should be abolished. We should be quite willing to abolish luxury, but to abolish honest, industrious, self-denying poverty would be to destroy the soil upon which mankind produces the virtues which enable our race to reach a still higher civilization than it now possesses.

I come now to the third step in my apprenticeship, for I had already taken two, as you see—the cotton factory and then the bobbin factory; and with the third—the third time is the chance, you know—deliverance came. I obtained a situation as messenger boy in the telegraph office of Pittsburgh when I was fourteen. Here I entered a new world.

Amid books, newspapers, pencils, pens and ink and writing-pads, and a clean office, bright windows, and the literary atmosphere, I was the happiest boy alive.

My only dread was that I should some day be dismissed because I did not know the city; for it is necessary that a messenger boy should know all the firms and addresses of men who are in the habit of receiving telegrams. But I was a stranger in Pittsburgh. However, I made up my mind that I would learn to repeat successively each business house in the principal streets, and was soon able to shut my eyes and begin at one side of Wood Street, and call every firm successively to the top, then pass to the other side and call every firm to the bottom. Before long I was able to do this with the business streets generally. My mind was then at rest upon that point.

Of course every messenger boy wants to become an operator, and before the operators arrive in the early mornings the boys slipped up to the instruments and practised. This I did, and was soon able to talk to the boys in the other offices along the line, who were also practising.

One morning I heard Philadelphia calling Pittsburgh

and giving the signal, "Death message." Great attention was then paid to "death messages," and I thought I ought to try to take this one. I answered and did so, and went off and delivered it before the operator came. After that the operators sometimes used to ask me to work for them.

Having a sensitive ear for sound, I soon learned to take messages by the ear, which was then very uncommon—I think only two persons in the United States could then do it. Now every operator takes by ear, so easy it is to follow and do what any other boy can—if you only have to. This brought me into notice, and finally I became an operator, and received the, to me, enormous recompense of twenty-five dollars per month—three hundred dollars a year!

This was a fortune—the very sum that I had fixed when I was a factory-worker as the fortune I wished to possess, because the family could live on three hundred dollars a year and be almost or quite independent. Here it was at last! But I was soon to be in receipt of extra compensation for extra work.

The six newspapers of Pittsburgh received telegraphic news in common. Six copies of each despatch were made by a gentleman who received six dollars per week for the work, and he offered me a gold dollar every week if I would do it, of which I was very glad indeed, because I always liked to work with news and scribble for newspapers.

The reporters came to a room every evening for the news which I had prepared, and this brought me into most pleasant intercourse with these clever fellows, and besides, I got a dollar a week as pocket-money, for this was not considered family revenue by me.

I think this last step of doing something beyond one's task is fully entitled to be considered "business." The other revenue, you see, was just salary obtained for regular work; but here was a little business operation upon my own account, and I was very proud indeed of my gold dollar every week.

The Pennsylvania Railroad shortly after this was completed to Pittsburgh, and that genius, Thomas A. Scott, was its superintendent. He often came to the telegraph office to talk to his chief, the general superintendent, at Altoona, and I became known to him in this way.

When that great railway system put up a wire of its own, he asked me to be his clerk and operator; so I left the telegraph office—in which there is great danger that a young man may be permanently buried, as it were—and became connected with the railways.

The new appointment was accompanied by what was, to me, a tremendous increase of salary. It jumped from twenty-five to thirty-five dollars per month. Mr. Scott was then receiving one hundred and twenty-five dollars per month, and I used to wonder what on earth he could do with so much money.

I remained for thirteen years in the service of the Pennsylvania Railroad Company, and was at last superintendent of the Pittsburgh division of the road, successor to Mr. Scott, who had in the meantime risen to the office of vice-president of the company.

One day Mr. Scott, who was the kindest of men, and had taken a great fancy to me, asked if I had or could find five hundred dollars to invest.

Here the business instinct came into play. I felt that as the door was opened for a business investment with my chief, it would be wilful flying in the face of providence if I did not jump at it; so I answered promptly:

"Yes, sir; I think I can."

"Very well," he said, "get it; a man has just died who owns ten shares in the Adams Express Company which I want you to buy. It will cost you fifty dollars per share, and I can help you with a little balance if you cannot raise it all."

Here was a queer position. The available assets of the whole family were not five hundred dollars. But there was one member of the family whose ability, pluck, and resource never failed us, and I felt sure the money could be raised somehow or other by my mother.

Indeed, had Mr. Scott known our position he would have advanced it himself; but the last thing in the world the proud Scot will do is to reveal his poverty and rely upon others. The family had managed by this time to purchase a small house and pay for it in order to save rent. My recollection is that it was worth eight hundred dollars.

The matter was laid before the council of three that night, and the oracle spoke: "Must be done. Mortgage our house. I will take the steamer in the morning for Ohio, and see uncle, and ask him to arrange it. I am sure he can." This was done. Of course her visit was successful—where did she ever fail?

The money was procured, paid over; ten shares of Adams Express Company stock was mine; but no one knew our little home had been mortgaged "to give our boy a start."

Adams Express stock then paid monthly dividends of one per cent, and the first check for five dollars arrived. I can see it now, and I well remember the signature of "J. C. Babcock, Cashier," who wrote a big "John Hancock" hand.

The next day being Sunday, we boys—myself and my ever-constant companions—took our usual Sunday afternoon stroll in the country, and sitting down in the woods, I showed them this check, saying, "Eureka! We have found it."

Here was something new to all of us, for none of us had ever received anything but from toil. A return from capital was something strange and new.

How money could make money, how, without any attention from me, this mysterious golden visitor should come, led to much speculation upon the part of the young fellows, and I was for the first time hailed as a "capitalist."

You see, I was beginning to serve my apprenticeship as a business man in a satisfactory manner.

A very important incident in my life occurred when,

one day in a train, a nice, farmer-looking gentleman approached me, saying that the conductor had told him I was connected with the Pennsylvania Railroad, and he would like to show me something. He pulled from a small green bag the model of the first sleeping-car. This was Mr. Woodruff, the inventor.

Its value struck me like a flash. I asked him to come to Altoona the following week, and he did so. Mr. Scott, with his usual quickness, grasped the idea. A contract was made with Mr. Woodruff to put two trial cars on the Pennsylvania Railroad. Before leaving Altoona Mr. Woodruff came and offered me an interest in the venture, which I promptly accepted. But how I was to make my payments rather troubled me, for the cars were to be paid for in monthly installments after delivery, and my first monthly payment was to be two hundred and seventeen dollars and a half.

I had not the money, and I did not see any way of getting it. But I finally decided to visit the local banker and ask him for a loan, pledging myself to repay at the rate of fifteen dollars per month. He promptly granted it. Never shall I forget his putting his arm over my shoulder, saying, "Oh, yes, Andy; you are all right!"

I then and there signed my first note. Proud day this; and surely now no one will dispute that I was becoming a "business man." I had signed my first note, and, most important of all—for any fellow can sign a note—I had found a banker willing to take it as "good."

My subsequent payments were made by the receipts from the sleeping-cars, and I really made my first considerable sum from this investment in the Woodruff Sleeping-car Company, which was afterward absorbed by Mr. Pullman— a remarkable man whose name is now known over all the world.

Shortly after this I was appointed superintendent of the Pittsburgh division, and returned to my dear old home, smoky Pittsburgh. Wooden bridges were then used exclusively upon the railways, and the Pennsylvania Railroad was experimenting with a bridge built of cast iron. I saw that wooden bridges would not do for the future, and organized a company in Pittsburgh to build iron bridges.

Here again I had recourse to the bank, because my share of the capital was twelve hundred and fifty dollars, and I had not the money; but the bank lent it to me, and we began the Keystone Bridge Works, which proved a great success. This company built the first great bridge over the Ohio River, three hundred feet span, and has built many of the most important structures since.

This was my beginning in manufacturing; and from that start all our other works have grown, the profits of one building the other. My "apprenticeship" as a business man soon ended, for I resigned my position as an officer of the Pennsylvania Railroad Company to give exclusive attention to business.

I was no longer merely an official working for others upon a salary, but a full-fledged business man working upon my own account.

I never was quite reconciled to working for other people. At the most, the railway officer has to look forward to the enjoyment of a stated salary, and he has a great many people to please; even if he gets to be president, he has sometimes a board of directors who cannot know what is best to be done; and even if this board be satisfied, he has a board of stockholders to criticize him, and as the property is not his own he cannot manage it as he pleases.

I always liked the idea of being my own master, of manufacturing something and giving employment to many men. There is only one thing to think of manufacturing if you are a Pittsburgher, for Pittsburgh even then had asserted her supremacy as the "Iron City," the leading iron-and-steel manufacturing city in America.

So my indispensable and clever partners, who had been

my boy companions, I am delighted to say—some of the very boys who had met in the grove to wonder at the five-dollar check—began business, and still continue extending it to meet the ever-growing and ever-changing wants of our most progressive country, year after year.

Always we are hoping that we need expand no farther; yet ever we are finding that to stop expanding would be to fall behind; and even today the successive improvements and inventions follow each other so rapidly that we see just as much yet to be done as ever.

When the manufacturer of steel ceases to grow he begins to decay, so we must keep on extending. The result of all these developments is that three pounds of finished steel are now bought in Pittsburgh for two cents, which is cheaper than anywhere else on the earth, and that our country has become the greatest producer of iron in the world.

And so ends the story of my apprenticeship and graduation as a business man.

The Martyr

A Story by Katherine Anne Porter

Rubén, the most illustrious painter in Mexico, was deeply in love with his model Isabel, who was in turn romantically attached to a rival artist whose name is of no importance.

Isabel used to call Rubén her little "Churro," which is a sort of sweet cake, and is, besides, a popular pet name among the Mexicans for small dogs. Rubén thought it a very delightful name, and would say before visitors to the studio, "And now she calls me 'Churro!' Ha! ha!" When he laughed, he shook in the waistcoat, for he was getting fat.

Then Isabel, who was tall and thin, with long, keen fingers, would rip her hands through a bouquet of flowers Rubén had brought her and scatter the petals, or she would cry, "Yah! yah!" derisively, and flick the tip of his nose with paint. She had been observed also to pull his hair and ears without mercy.

When earnest-minded people made pilgrimages down the narrow, cobbled street, picked their way carefully over puddles in the patio, and clattered up the uncertain stairs for a glimpse of the great and yet so simple personage, she would cry, "Here come the pretty sheep!" She enjoyed their gaze of wonder at her daring.

Often she was bored, for sometimes she would stand all day long, braiding and unbraiding her hair while Rubén made sketches of her, and they would forget to eat until late; but there was no place for her to go until her lover,

Katherine Anne Porter was drawn to a life of adventure, but chose to associate with artists. In The Martyr, *however, the murderer is a tamale, not Art.*

Rubén's rival, should sell a painting, for everyone declared Rubén would kill on sight the man who even attempted to rob him of Isabel. So Isabel stayed, and Rubén made eighteen different drawings of her for his mural, and she cooked for him occasionally, quarreled with him, and put out her long, red tongue at visitors she did not like. Rubén adored her.

He was just beginning the nineteenth drawing of Isabel when his rival sold a very large painting to a rich man whose decorator told him he must have a panel of green and orange on a certain wall of his new house. By a felicitous chance, this painting was prodigiously green and orange. The rich man paid him a huge price, but was happy to do it, he explained, because it would cost six times as much to cover the space with tapestry. The rival was happy, too, though he neglected to explain why. The next day he and Isabel went to Costa Rica, and that is the end of them so far as we are concerned.

Rubén read her farewell note:

"Poor old Churro! It is a pity your life is so very dull, and I cannot live it any longer. I am going away with someone who will never allow me to cook for him, but will make a mural with fifty figures of me in it, instead of only twenty. I am also to have red slippers, and a gay life to my heart's content.

"Your old friend, Isabel."

When Rubén read this, he felt like a man drowning. His breath would not come, and he thrashed his arms about a great deal. Then he drank a large bottle of *tequila*, without lemon or salt to take the edge off, and lay down on the floor with his head in a palette of freshly mixed paint and wept vehemently.

After this, he was altogether a changed man. He could not talk unless he was telling about Isabel, her angelic face, her pretty little tricks and ways: "She used to kick my shins black and blue," he would say, fondly, and the tears would flow into his eyes. He was always eating crisp sweet cakes from a bag near his easel. "See," he would say, holding one up before taking a mouthful, "she used to call me 'Churro,' like this!"

His friends were all pleased to see Isabel go, and said among themselves he was lucky to lose the lean she-devil. They set themselves to help him forget. But Rubén could not be distracted. "There is no other woman like that woman," he would say, shaking his head stubbornly. "When she went, she took my life with her. I have no spirit even for revenge." Then he would add, "I tell you, my poor little angel Isabel is a murderess, for she has broken my heart."

At times he would roam anxiously about the studio, kicking his felt slippers into the shuffles of drawings piled about, gathering dust, or he would grind colors for a few minutes, saying in a dolorous voice: "She once did all this for me. Imagine her goodness!" But always he came back to the window, and ate sweets and fruits and almond cakes from the bag. When his friends took him out for dinner, he would sit quietly and eat huge platefuls of every sort of food, and wash it down with sweet wine. Then he would begin to weep, and talk about Isabel.

His friends agreed it was getting rather stupid. Isabel had been gone for nearly six months, and Rubén refused even to touch the nineteenth figure of her, much less to begin the twentieth, and the mural was getting nowhere.

"Look, my dear friend," said Ramón, who did caricatures, and heads of pretty girls for the magazines, "even I, who am not a great artist, know how women can spoil a man's work for him. Let me tell you, when Trinidad left me, I was good for nothing for a week. Nothing tasted properly, I could not tell one color from another, I positively was tone deaf. That shameless cheat-by-night almost ruined me. But you, *amigo,* rouse yourself, and finish your great mural for the world, for the future, and remember Isabel only when you give thanks to God that she is gone."

Rubén would shake his head as he sat collapsed upon his couch munching sugared almonds, and would cry:

"I have a pain in my heart that will kill me. There is no woman like that one."

His collars suddenly refused to meet under his chin. He loosened his belt three notches, and explained: "I sit still; I cannot move any more. My energy has gone to grief." The layers of fat piled insidiously upon him, he bulged until he became strange even to himself. Ramón, showing his new caricature of Rubén to his friends, declared: "I could as well have drawn it with a compass, I swear. The buttons are bursting from his shirt. It is positively unsafe."

But still Rubén sat, eating moodily in solitude, and weeping over Isabel after his third bottle of sweet wine at night.

His friends talked it over, concluded that the affair was growing desperate; it was high time someone should tell him the true cause of his pain. But everyone wished the other would be the one chosen. And it came out there was not a person in the group, possibly not one in all Mexico, indelicate enough to do such a thing. They decided to shift the responsibility upon a physician from the faculty of the university. In the mind of such a one would be combined a sufficiently refined sentiment with the highest degree of technical knowledge. This was the diplomatic, the discreet, the fastidious thing to do. It was done.

The doctor found Rubén seated before his easel, facing the half-finished nineteenth figure of Isabel. He was weeping, and between sobs he ate spoonfuls of soft Toluca cheese, with spiced mangos. He hung in all directions over his painting-stool, like a mound of kneaded dough. He told the doctor first about Isabel. "I do assure you faithfully, my friend, not even I could capture in paint the line of beauty in her thigh and instep. And, besides, she was an angel for kindness." Later he said the pain in his heart would be the death of him. The doctor was profoundly touched. For a great while he sat offering consolation without courage to prescribe material cures for a man of such delicately adjusted susceptibilities.

"I have only crass and vulgar remedies"—with a graceful gesture he seemed to offer them between thumb and forefinger—"but they are all the world of flesh may contribute toward the healing of the wounded spirit." He named them one at a time. They made a neat, but not impressive, row: a diet, fresh air, long walks, frequent violent exercise, preferably on the cross-bar, ice showers, almost no wine.

Rubén seemed not to hear him. His sustained, oblivious murmur flowed warmly through the doctor's solemnly rounded periods:

"The pains are most unendurable at night, when I lie in my lonely bed and gaze at the empty heavens through my narrow window, and I think to myself, 'Soon my grave shall be narrower than that window, and darker than that firmament,' and my heart gives a writhe. Ah, Isabelita, my executioner!"

The doctor tiptoed out respectfully, and left him sitting there eating cheese and gazing with wet eyes at the nineteenth figure of Isabel.

The friends grew hopelessly bored and left him more and more alone. No one saw him for some weeks except the proprietor of a small cafe called "The Little Monkeys" where Rubén was accustomed to dine with Isabel and where he now went alone for food.

Here one night quite suddenly Rubén clasped his heart with violence, rose from his chair, and upset the dish of tamales and pepper gravy he had been eating. The proprietor ran to him. Rubén said something in a hurried whisper, made rather an impressive gesture over his head with one arm, and, to say it as gently as possible, died.

His friends hastened the next day to see the proprietor, who gave them a solidly dramatic version of the lamentable episode.

Ramón was even then gathering material for an intimate biography of his country's most eminent painter, to be illustrated with large numbers of his own character portraits. Already the dedication was composed to his "Friend and Master, Inspired and Incomparable Genius of Art on the American Continent."

"But what did he say to you," insisted Ramón, "at the final stupendous moment? It is most important. The last words of a great artist, they should be very eloquent. Repeat them precisely, my dear fellow! It will add splendor to the biography, nay, to the very history of art itself, if they are eloquent."

The proprietor nodded his head with the air of a man who understands everything.

"I know, I know. Well, maybe you will not believe me when I tell you that his very last words were a truly sublime message to you, his good and faithful friends, and to the world. He said, gentlemen: 'Tell them I am a martyr to love. I perish in a cause worthy the sacrifice. I die of a broken heart!' and then he said, 'Isabelita, my executioner!' That was all, gentlemen," ended the proprietor, simply and reverently. He bowed his head. They all bowed their heads.

"That was truly magnificent," said Ramón, after the correct interval of silent mourning. "I thank you. It is a superb epitaph. I am most gratified."

"He was also supremely fond of my tamales and pepper gravy," added the proprietor in a modest tone. "They were his final indulgence."

"That shall be mentioned in its place, never fear, my good friend," cried Ramón, his voice crumbling with generous emotion, "with the name of your cafe, even. It shall be a shrine for artists when this story is known. Trust me faithfully to preserve for the future every smallest detail in the life and character of this great genius. Each episode has its own sacred, its precious and peculiar interest. Yes, truly, I shall mention the tamales."

A Horseman in the Sky

A Story by Ambrose Bierce

ONE sunny afternoon in the autumn of the year 1861 a soldier lay in a clump of laurel by the side of a road in western Virginia. He lay at full length upon his stomach, his feet resting upon the toes, his head upon the left fore-arm. His extended right hand loosely grasped his rifle. But for the somewhat methodical disposition of his limbs and a slight rhythmic movement of the cartridge box at the back of his belt he might have been thought to be dead. He was asleep at his post of duty. But if detected he would be dead shortly afterward, death being the just and legal penalty of his crime.

The clump of laurel in which the criminal lay was in the angle of a road which after ascending southward a steep acclivity to that point turned sharply to the west, running along the summit for perhaps one hundred yards. There it turned southward again and went zigzagging downward through the forest. At the salient of that second angle was a large flat rock, jutting out northward, overlooking the deep valley from which the road ascended. The rock capped a high cliff; a stone dropped from its outer edge would have fallen sheer downward one thousand feet to the tops of the pines. The angle where the soldier lay was on another spur of the same cliff. Had he been awake he would have com-manded a view, not only of the short arm of the road and the jutting rock, but of the entire profile of the cliff below it. It might well have made him giddy to look.

The mysterious nature of Ambrose Bierce's death, as he attempted a rendevous with Pancho Villa, has not prevented him from sliding into undeserved obscurity.

The country was wooded everywhere except at the bottom of the valley to the northward, where there was a small natural meadow, through which flowed a stream scarcely visible from the valley's rim. This open ground looked hardly larger than an ordinary dooryard, but was really several acres in extent. Its green was more vivid than that of the inclosing forest. Away beyond it rose a line of giant cliffs similar to those upon which we are supposed to stand in our survey of the savage scene, and through which the road had somehow made its climb to the summit. The configuration of the valley, indeed, was such that from this point of observation it seemed entirely shut in, and one could but have wondered how the road which found a way out of it had found a way into it, and whence came and whither went the waters of the stream that parted the meadow more than a thousand feet below.

No country is so wild and difficult but men will make it a theater of war; concealed in the forest at the bottom of that military rattrap, in which half a hundred men in possession of the exits might have starved an army to submission, lay five regiments of Federal infantry. They had marched all the previous day and night and were resting. At nightfall they would take to the road again, climb to the place where their faithful sentinel now slept, and descending the other slope of the ridge fall upon a camp of the enemy at about midnight. Their hope was to surprise it, for the road led to the rear of it. In case of failure, their position would be perilous in the extreme; and fail they surely would should accident or vigilance apprise the enemy of the movement.

The sleeping sentinel in the clump of laurel was a young Virginian named Carter Druse. He was the son of wealthy parents, an only child, and had known such ease and cultivation and high living as wealth and taste were able to command in the mountain country of western Virginia. His home was but a few miles from where he now lay. One morning he had risen from the breakfast table and said, quietly but gravely: "Father, a Union regiment has arrived at Grafton. I am going to join it."

The father lifted his leonine head, looked at the son a moment in silence, and replied: "Well, go, sir, and whatever may occur do what you conceive to be your duty. Virginia, to which you are a traitor, must get on without you. Should we both live to the end of the war we will speak further of the matter. Your mother, as the physician has informed you, is in a most critical condition; at the best she cannot be with us longer than a few weeks, but that time is precious. It would be better not to disturb her."

So Carter Druse, bowing reverently to his father, who returned the salute with a stately courtesy that masked a breaking heart, left the home of his childhood to go soldiering. By conscience and courage, by deeds of devotion and daring, he soon commended himself to his fellows and his officers; and it was to these qualities and to some knowledge of the country that he owed his selection for his present perilous duty at the extreme outpost. Nevertheless, fatigue had been stronger than resolution and he had fallen asleep. What good or bad angel came in a dream to rouse him from his state of crime, who shall say? Without a movement, without a sound, in the profound silence and the languor of the late afternoon some invisible messenger of fate touched with unsealing finger the eyes of his consciousness—whispered into the ear of his spirit the mysterious awakening word which no human lips ever have spoken, no human memory ever has recalled. He quietly raised his forehead from his arm and looked between the masking stems of the laurels, instinctively closing his right hand about the stock of his rifle.

His first feeling was a keen artistic delight. On a colossal pedestal, the cliff—motionless at the extreme edge of the capping rock, and sharply outlined against the sky—

was an equestrian statue of impressive dignity. The figure of the man sat the figure of the horse, straight and soldierly, but with the repose of a Grecian god carved in the marble which limits the suggestion of activity. The gray costume harmonized with its aerial background; the metal of accouterment and caparison was softened and subdued by the shadow; the animal's skin had no points of high light. A carbine strikingly foreshortened lay across the pommel of the saddle, kept in place by the right hand grasping it at the "grip"; the left hand, holding the bridle rein, was invisible. In silhouette against the sky the profile of the horse was cut with the sharpness of a cameo; it looked across the heights of air to the confronting cliffs beyond. The face of the rider, turned slightly away, showed only an outline of temple and beard; he was looking downward to the bottom of the valley. Magnified by its lift against the sky and by the soldier's testifying sense of the formidableness of a near enemy the group appeared of heroic, almost colossal, size.

For an instant Druse had a strange, half-defined feeling that he had slept to the end of the war and was looking upon a noble work of art reared upon that eminence to commemorate the deeds of an heroic past of which he had been an inglorious part. The feeling was dispelled by a slight movement of the group: the horse, without moving its feet, had drawn its body slightly backward from the verge; the man remained immobile as before. Broad awake and keenly alive to the significance of the situation, Druse now brought the butt of his rifle against his cheek by cautiously pushing the barrel forward through the bushes, cocked the piece, and glancing through the sights covered a vital spot of the horseman's breast. A touch upon the trigger and all would have been well with Carter Druse. At that instant the horseman turned his head and looked in the direction of his concealed foeman—seemed to look into his very face, into his eyes, into his brave, compassionate heart.

Is it then so terrible to kill an enemy in war—an enemy who has surprised a secret vital to the safety of one's self and comrades—an enemy more formidable for his knowledge than all his army for its numbers? Carter Druse grew pale; he shook in every limb, turned faint, and saw the statuesque group before him as black figures, rising, falling, moving unsteadily in arcs of circles in a fiery sky. His hand fell away from his weapon, his head slowly dropped until his face rested on the leaves in which he lay. This courageous gentleman and hardy soldier was near swooning from intensity of emotion.

It was not for long; in another moment his face was raised from earth, his hands resumed their places on the rifle, his forefinger sought the trigger; mind, heart, and eyes were clear, conscience and reason sound. He could not hope to capture that enemy; to alarm him would but send him dashing to his camp with his fatal news. The duty of the soldier was plain: the man must be shot dead from ambush—without warning, without a moment's spiritual preparation, with never so much as an unspoken prayer, he must be sent to his account. But no—there is a hope—he may have discovered nothing—perhaps he is but admiring the sublimity of the landscape. If permitted, he may turn and ride carelessly away in the direction whence he came. Surely it will be possible to judge at the instant of his withdrawing whether he knows. It may well be that his fixity of attention—Druse turned his head and looked through the deeps of air downward, as from the surface to the bottom of a translucent sea. He saw creeping across the green meadow a sinuous line of figures of men and horses—some foolish commander was permitting the soldiers of his escort to water their beasts in the open, in plain view from a dozen summits!

Druse withdrew his eyes from the valley and fixed them again upon the group of man and horse in the sky, and again it was through the sights of his rifle. But this time his aim was at the horse. In his memory, as if they were a divine mandate, rang the words of his father at their parting: "Whatever may occur, do what you conceive to be your duty." He was calm now. His teeth were firmly but not rigidly closed; his nerves were as tranquil as a sleeping babe's—not a tremor affected any muscle of his body; his breathing, until suspended in the act of taking aim, was regular and slow. Duty had conquered; the spirit had said to the body: "Peace, be still." He fired.

An officer of the Federal force who in a spirit of adventure or in quest of knowledge had left the hidden bivouac in the valley, and with aimless feet had made his way to the lower edge of a small open space near the foot of the cliff, was considering what he had to gain by pushing his exploration further. At a distance of a quarter mile before him, but apparently at a stone's throw, rose from its fringe of pines the gigantic face of rock, towering to so great a height above him that it made him giddy to look up to where its edge cut a sharp, rugged line against the sky. It presented a clean, vertical profile against a background of blue sky to a point half the way down, and of distant hills hardly less blue, thence to the tops of the trees at its base. Lifting his eyes to the dizzy altitude of its summit the officer saw an astonishing sight—a man on horseback riding down into the valley through the air.

Straight upright sat the rider, in military fashion, with a firm seat in the saddle, a strong clutch upon the rein to hold his charger from too impetuous a plunge. From his bare head his long hair streamed upward, waving like a plume. His hands were concealed in the cloud of the horse's lifted mane. The animal's body was as level as if every hoof stroke encountered the resistant earth. Its motions were those of a wild gallop, but even as the officer looked they ceased, with all the legs thrown sharply forward as in the act of alighting from a leap.

But this was a flight!

Filled with amazement and terror by this apparition of a horseman in the sky—half believing himself the chosen scribe of some new Apocalypse, the officer was overcome by the intensity of his emotions; his legs failed him and he fell. Almost at the same instant he heard a crashing sound in the trees—a sound that died without an echo—and all was still.

The officer rose to his feet, trembling. The familiar sensation of an abraded shin recalled his dazed faculties. Pulling himself together he ran rapidly obliquely away from the cliff to a point distant from its foot; thereabout he expected to find his man; and thereabout he naturally failed. In the fleeting instant of his vision his imagination had been so wrought upon by the apparent grace and ease and intention of the marvelous performance that it did not occur to him that the line of march of aerial cavalry is directly downward, and that he could find the objects of his search at the very foot of the cliff. A half-hour later he returned to camp.

This officer was a wise man; he knew better than to tell an incredible truth. He said nothing of what he had seen. But when the commander asked him if in his scout he had learned anything of advantage to the expedition he answered:

"Yes, sir—there is no road leading down into this valley from the southward."

The commander, knowing better, smiled.

After firing his shot, Private Carter Druse reloaded his rifle and resumed his watch. Ten minutes had hardly passed when a Federal sergeant crept cautiously to him on hands and knees. Druse neither turned his head nor looked at him, but lay without motion or sign of recognition.

"Did you fire?" tbe sergeant whispered.

"Yes."

"At what?"

"A horse. It was standing on yonder rock—pretty far out. You see it is no longer there. It went over the cliff."

The man's face was white, but he showed no other sign of emotion. Having answered, he turned away his eyes and said no more. The sergeant did not understand.

"See here, Druse," he said, after a moment's silence, "it's no use making a mystery. I order you to report. Was there anybody on the horse?"

"Yes."

"Well?"

"My father."

The sergeant rose to his feet and walked away. "Good God!" he said.

The Celestial Omnibus

A Story by E.M. Forster

THE boy who resided at Agathox Lodge, 28, Bucking-ham Park Road, Surbiton, had often been puzzled by the old sign-post that stood almost opposite. He asked his mother about it, and she replied that it was a joke, and not a very nice one, which had been made many years back by some naughty young men, and that the police ought to re-move it. For there were two strange things about this sign-post: firstly, it pointed up a blank alley, and, secondly, it had painted on it, in faded characters, the words, "To Heaven."

"What kind of young men were they?" he asked.

"I think your father told me that one of them wrote verses, and was expelled from the University and came to grief in other ways. Still, it was a long time ago. You must ask your father about it. He will say the same as I do, that it was put up as a joke."

"So it doesn't mean anything at all?"

She sent him up-stairs to put on his best things, for the Bonses were coming to tea, and he was to hand the cake-stand.

It struck him, as he wrenched on his tightening trou-sers, that he might do worse than ask Mr. Bons about the sign-post. His father, though very kind, always laughed at him—shrieked with laughter whenever he or any other child asked a question or spoke. But Mr. Bons was serious

> *E.M. Forster wrote some of the finest stories of pure fantasy in English literature. This one reminds us of the horror of a closed mind.*

as well as kind. He had a beautiful house and lent one books, he was a churchwarden, and a candidate for the County Council; he had donated to the Free Library enormously, he presided over the Literary Society, and had Members of Parliament to stop with him—in short, he was probably the wisest person alive.

Yet even Mr. Bons could only say that the signpost was a joke—the joke of a person named Shelley.

"Of course!" cried the mother; "I told you so, dear. That was the name."

"Had you never heard of Shelley?" asked Mr. Bons.

"No," said the boy, and hung his head.

"But is there no Shelley in the house?"

"Why, yes!" exclaimed the lady, in much agitation. "Dear Mr. Bons, we aren't such Philistines as that. Two at the least. One a wedding present, and the other, smaller print, in one of the spare rooms."

"I believe we have seven Shelleys," said Mr. Bons, with a slow smile. Then he brushed the cake crumbs off his stomach, and, together with his daughter, rose to go.

The boy, obeying a wink from his mother, saw them all the way to the garden gate, and when they had gone he did not at once return to the house, but gazed for a little up and down Buckingham Park Road.

His parents lived at the right end of it. After No. 39 the quality of the houses dropped very suddenly, and 64 had not even a separate servants' entrance. But at the present moment the whole road looked rather pretty, for the sun had just set in splendour, and the inequalities of rent were drowned in a saffron afterglow. Small birds twittered, and the breadwinners' train shrieked musically down through the cutting—that wonderful cutting which has drawn to itself the whole beauty out of Surbiton, and clad itself, like any Alpine valley, with the glory of the fir and the silver birch and the primrose. It was this cutting that had first stirred desires within the boy—desires for something just a little different, he knew not what, desires that would return whenever things were sunlit, as they were this evening, running up and down inside him, up and down, up and down, till he would feel quite unusual all over, and as likely as not would want to cry. This evening he was even sillier, for he slipped across the road towards the sign-post and began to run up the blank alley.

The alley runs between high walls—the walls of the gardens of "Ivanhoe" and "Belle Vista" respectively. It smells a little all the way, and is scarcely twenty yards long, including the turn at the end. So not unnaturally the boy soon came to a standstill. "I'd like to kick that Shelley," he exclaimed, and glanced idly at a piece of paper which was pasted on the wall. Rather an odd piece of paper, and he read it carefully before he turned back. This is what he read:

S. AND C. R. C. C.
Alteration in Service.

Owing to lack of patronage the Company are regretfully compelled to suspend the hourly service, and to retain only the

Sunrise and Sunset Omnibuses,

which will run as usual. It is to be hoped that the public will patronize an arrangement which is intended for their convenience. As an extra inducement, the Company will, for the first time, now issue

Return Tickets!

(available one day only), which may be obtained of the driver. Passengers are again reminded that *no tickets are issued at the other end,* and that no complaints in this connection will receive consideration from the

Company. Nor will the Company be responsible for any negligence or stupidity on the part of Passengers, nor for Hailstorms, Lightning, Loss of Tickets, nor for any Act of God.

☙ For the Direction.

Now he had never seen this notice before, nor could he imagine where the omnibus went to. S, of course was for Surbiton, and R.C.C. meant Road Car Company. But what was the meaning of the other C.? Coombe and Malden, perhaps, or possibly "City." Yet it could not hope to compete with the SouthWestern. The whole thing, the boy reflected, was run on hopelessly unbusiness-like lines. Why no tickets from the other end? And what an hour to start! Then he realized that unless the notice was a hoax, an omnibus must have been starting just as he was wishing the Bonses good-bye. He peered at the ground through the gathering dusk, and there he saw what might or might not be the marks of wheels. Yet nothing had come out of the alley. And he had never seen an omnibus at any time in the Buckingham Park Road. No: it must be a hoax, like the sign-posts, like the fairy tales, like the dreams upon which he would wake suddenly in the night. And with a sigh he stepped from the alley— right into the arms of his father.

Oh, how his father laughed! "Poor, poor Popsey!" he cried. "Diddums! Diddums! Diddums think he'd walky-palky up to Evvink!" And his mother, also convulsed with laughter, appeared on the steps of Agathox Lodge. "Don't Bob!" she gasped. "Don't be so naughty! Oh, you'll kill me! Oh, leave the boy alone!"

But all the evening the joke was kept up. The father implored to be taken too. Was it a very tiring walk? Need one wipe one's shoes on the door-mat? And the boy went to bed feeling faint and sore, and thankful for only one thing— that he had not said a word about the omnibus. It was a hoax, yet through his dreams it grew more and more real, and the streets of Surbiton, through which he saw it driving, seemed instead to become hoaxes and shadows. And very early in the morning he woke with a cry, for he had had a glimpse of its destination.

He struck a match, and its light fell not only on his watch but also on his calendar, so that he knew it to be half-an-hour to sunrise. It was pitch dark, for the fog had come down from London in the night, and all Surbiton was wrapped in its embraces. Yet he sprang out and dressed himself, for he was determined to settle once for all which was real: the omnibus or the streets. "I shall be a fool one way or the other," he thought, "until I know." Soon he was shivering in the road under the gas lamp that guarded the entrance to the alley.

To enter the alley itself required some courage. Not only was it horribly dark, but he now realized that it was an impossible terminus for an omnibus. If it had not been for a policeman, whom he heard approaching through the fog, he would never have made the attempt. The next moment he had made the attempt and failed. Nothing. Nothing but a blank alley and a very silly boy gaping at its dirty floor. It was a hoax. "I'll tell papa and mamma," he decided. "I deserve it. I deserve that they should know. I am too silly to be alive." And he went back to the gate of Agathox Lodge.

There he remembered that his watch was fast. The sun was not risen; it would not rise for two minutes. "Give the bus every chance," he thought cynically, and returned into the alley.

But the omnibus was there.

It had two horses, whose sides were still smoking from their journey, and its two great lamps shone through the fog against the alley's walls, changing their cobwebs and moss into tissues of fairyland. The driver was huddled up in a cape. He faced the blank wall, and how he had managed to drive in so neatly and so silently was one of the many things that the boy never discovered. Nor could he imagine how ever he would drive out.

"Please," his voice quavered through the foul brown air, "Please, is that an omnibus?"

"Omnibus est," said the driver, without turning round. There was a moment's silence. The policeman passed, coughing, by the entrance of the alley. The boy crouched in the shadow, for he did not want to be found out. He was pretty sure, too, that it was a Pirate; nothing else, he reasoned, would go from such odd places and at such odd hours.

"About when do you start?" He tried to sound nonchalant.

"At sunrise."

"How far do you go?"

"The whole way."

"And can I have a return ticket which will bring me all the way back?"

"You can."

"Do you know, I half think I'll come." The driver made no answer. The sun must have risen, for he unhitched the brake. And scarcely had the boy jumped in before the omnibus was off.

How? Did it turn? There was no room. Did it go forward? There was a blank wall. Yet it was moving—moving at a stately pace through the fog, which had turned from brown to yellow. The thought of warm bed and warmer breakfast made the boy feel faint. He wished he had not come. His parents would not have approved. He would have gone back to them if the weather had not made it impossible. The solitude was terrible; he was the only passenger. And the omnibus, though well built, was cold and somewhat musty. He drew his coat round him, and in so doing chanced to feel his pocket. It was empty. He had forgotten his purse.

"Stop!" he shouted. "Stop!" And then, being of a polite disposition, he glanced up at the painted notice-board so that he might call the driver by name. "Mr. Browne! stop; O, do please stop!"

Mr. Browne did not stop, but he opened a little window and looked in at the boy. His face was a surprise, so kind it was and modest.

"Mr. Browne, I've left my purse behind. I've not got a penny. I can't pay for the ticket. Will you take my watch, please? I am in the most awful hole."

"Tickets on this line," said the driver, "whether single or return, can be purchased by coinage from no terrene mint. And a chronometer, though it had solaced the vigils of Charlemagne, or measured the slumbers of Laura, can acquire by no mutation the double-cake that charms the fangless Cerberus of Heaven!" So saying, he handed in the necessary ticket, and, while the boy said "Thank you," continued: "Titular pretensions, I know it well, are vanity. Yet they merit no censure when uttered on a laughing lip, and in an homonymous world are in some sort useful, since they do serve to distinguish one Jack from his fellow. Remember me, therefore, as Sir Thomas Browne."

"Are you a Sir? Oh, sorry!" He had heard of these gentlemen drivers. "It is good of you about the ticket. But if you go on at this rate, however does your bus pay?"

"It does not pay. It was not intended to pay. Many are the faults of my equipage; it is compounded too curiously of foreign woods; its cushions tickle erudition rather than promote repose; and my horses are nourished not on the evergreen pastures of the moment, but on the dried bents and clovers of Latinity. But that it pays!—that error at all events was never intended and never attained."

"Sorry again," said the boy rather hopelessly. Sir Thomas looked sad, fearing that, even for a moment, he had been the cause of sadness. He invited the boy to come up and sit beside him on the box, and together they journeyed on through the fog, which was now changing from yellow to white. There were no houses by the road; so it must be either Putney Heath or Wimbledon Common.

"Have you been a driver always?"

"I was a physician once."

"But why did you stop? Weren't you good?"

"As a healer of bodies I had scant success, and several score of my patients preceded me. But as a healer of the spirit I have succeeded beyond my hopes and my deserts. For though my draughts were not better nor subtler than those of other men, yet, by reason of the cunning goblets wherein I offered them, the queasy soul was ofttimes tempted to sip and be refreshed."

"The queasy soul," he murmured; "if the sun sets with trees in front of it, and you suddenly come strange all over, is that a queasy soul?"

"Have you felt that?"

"Why yes."

After a pause he told the boy a little, a very little, about the journey's end. But they did not chatter much, for the boy, when he liked a person, would as soon sit silent in his company as speak, and this, he discovered, was also the mind of Sir Thomas Browne and of many others with whom he was to be acquainted. He heard, however, about the young man Shelley, who was now quite a famous person, with a carriage of his own, and about some of the other drivers who are in the service of the Company. Meanwhile the light grew stronger, though the fog did not disperse. It was now more like mist than fog, and at times would travel quickly across them, as if it was part of a cloud. They had been ascending, too, in a most puzzling way; for over two hours the horses had been pulling against the collar, and even if it were Richmond Hill they ought to have been at the top long ago. Perhaps it was Epsom, or even the North Downs; yet the air seemed keener than that which blows on either. And as to the name of their destination, Sir Thomas Browne was silent.

Crash!

"Thunder, by Jove!" said the boy, "and not so far off either. Listen to the echoes! It's more like mountains."

He thought, not very vividly, of his father and mother. He saw them sitting down to sausages and listening to the storm. He saw his own empty place. Then there would be questions, alarms, theories, jokes, consolations. They would expect him back at lunch. To lunch he would not come, nor to tea, but he would be in for dinner, and so his day's truancy would be over. If he had had his purse he would have bought them presents—not that he should have known what to get them.

Crash!

The peal and the lightning came together. The cloud quivered as if it were alive, and torn streamers of mist rushed past. "Are you afraid?" asked Sir Thomas Browne.

"What is there to be afraid of? Is it much farther?"

The horses of the omnibus stopped just as a ball of fire burst up and exploded with a ringing noise that was deafening but clear, like the noise of a blacksmith's forge. All the cloud was shattered.

"Oh, listen, Sir Thomas Browne! No, I mean look; we shall get a view at last. No, I mean listen; that sounds like a rainbow!"

The noise had died into the faintest murmur, beneath which another murmur grew, spreading stealthily, steadily, in a curve that widened but did not vary. And in widening curves a rainbow was spreading from the horses' feet into the dissolving mists.

"But how beautiful! What colours! Where will it stop? It is more like the rainbows you can tread on. More like dreams."

The colour and the sound grew together. The rainbow spanned an enormous gulf. Clouds rushed under it and were pierced by it, and still it grew, reaching forward, conquering the darkness, until it touched something that seemed more solid than a cloud.

The boy stood up. "What is that out there?" he called. "What does it rest on, out at that other end?"

In the morning sunshine a precipice shone forth beyond the gulf. A precipice—or was it a castle? The horses moved. They set their feet upon the rainbow.

"Oh, look!" the boy shouted. "Oh, listen! Those caves— or are they gateways? Oh, look between those cliffs at those ledges. I see people! I see trees!"

"Look also below," whispered Sir Thomas. "Neglect not the diviner Acheron."

The boy looked below, past the flames of the rainbow that licked against their wheels. The gulf also had cleared, and in its depths there flowed an everlasting river. One sunbeam entered and struck a green pool, and as they passed over he saw three maidens rise to the surface of the pool, singing, and playing with something that glistened like a ring.

"You down in the water," he called.

They answered, "You up on the bridge—" There was a burst of music. "You up on the bridge, good luck to you. Truth in the depth, truth on the height."

"You down in the water, what are you doing?"

Sir Thomas Browne replied: "They sport in the mancipiary possession of their gold"; and the omnibus arrived.

The boy was in disgrace. He sat locked up in the nursery of Agathox Lodge, learning poetry for a punishment. His father had said, "My boy! I can pardon anything but untruthfulness," and had caned him, saying at each stroke, "There is *no* omnibus, *no* driver, *no* bridge, *no* mountain; you are a truant, a *gutter snipe,* a *liar.*" His father could be very stern at times. His mother had begged him to say he was sorry. But he could not say that. It was the greatest day of his life, in spite of the caning and the poetry at the end of it.

He had returned punctually at sunset—driven not by Sir Thomas Browne, but by a maiden lady who was full of quiet fun. They had talked of omnibuses and also of barouche landaus. How far away her gentle voice seemed now! Yet it was scarcely three hours since he had left her up the alley.

His mother called through the door. "Dear, you are to come down and to bring your poetry with you."

He came down, and found that Mr. Bons was in the smoking-room with his father. It had been a dinner party.

"Here is the great traveller!" said his father grimly. "Here is the young gentleman who drives in an omnibus over rainbows, while young ladies sing to him." Pleased with his wit, he laughed.

"After all," said Mr. Bons, smiling, "there is something a little like it in Wagner. It is odd how, in quite illiterate minds, you will find glimmers of Artistic Truth. The case interests me. Let me plead for the culprit. We have all romanced in our time, haven't we?"

"Hear how kind Mr. Bons is," said his mother, while his father said, "Very well. Let him say his Poem, and that will do. He is going away to my sister on Tuesday, and *she* will cure him of this alley-slopering." (Laughter.) "Say your Poem."

The boy began. " 'Standing aloof in giant ignorance.' "

His father laughed again—roared. "One for you, my son! 'Standing aloof in giant ignorance!' I never knew these poets talked sense. Just describes you. Here, Bons, you go in for poetry. Put him through it, will you, while I fetch up the whisky?"

"Yes, give me the Keats," said Mr. Bons. "Let him say his Keats to me."

So for a few moments the wise man and the ignorant boy were left alone in the smoking-room.

" 'Standing aloof in giant ignorance, of thee I dream and of the Cyclades, as one who sits ashore and longs perchance to visit—' "

"Quite right. To visit what?"

" 'To visit dolphin coral in deep seas,' " said the boy, and burst into tears.

"Come, come! why do you cry?"

"Because—because all these words that only rhymed before, now that I've come back they're me."

Mr. Bons laid the Keats down. The case was more interesting than he had expected. *"You!"* he exclaimed. "This sonnet, *you?"*

"Yes—and look further on: 'Aye, on the shores of darkness there is light, and precipices show untrodden green.' It *is* so, sir. All these things are true."

"I never doubted it," said Mr. Bons, with closed eyes.

"You—then you believe me? You believe in the omnibus and the driver and the storm and that return ticket I got for nothing and—"

"Tut, tut! No more of your yarns, my boy. I meant that I never doubted the essential truth of Poetry. Some day, when you have read more, you will understand what I mean."

"But Mr. Bons, it *is* so. There *is* light upon the shores of darkness. I have seen it coming. Light and a wind."

"Nonsense," said Mr. Bons.

"If I had stopped! They tempted me. They told me to give up my ticket—for you cannot come back if you lose your ticket. They called from the river for it, and indeed I was tempted, for I have never been so happy as among those precipices. But I thought of my mother and father, and that I must fetch them. Yet they will not come, though the road starts opposite our house. It has all happened as the people up there warned me, and Mr. Bons has disbelieved me like every one else. I have been caned. I shall never see that mountain again."

"What's that about me?" said Mr. Bons, sitting up in his chair very suddenly.

"I told them about you, and how clever you were, and

how many books you had, and they said, 'Mr. Bons will certainly disbelieve you.' "

"Stuff and nonsense, my young friend. You grow impertinent. I—well—I will settle the matter. Not a word to your father. I will cure you. To-morrow evening I will myself call here to take you for a walk, and at sunset we will go up this alley opposite and hunt for your omnibus, you silly little boy."

His face grew serious, for the boy was not disconcerted, but leapt about the room singing, "Joy! joy! I told them you would believe me. We will drive together over the rainbow. I told them that you would come." After all, could there be anything in the story? Wagner? Keats? Shelley? Sir Thomas Browne? Certainly the case was interesting.

And on the morrow evening, though it was pouring with rain, Mr. Bons did not omit to call at Agathox Lodge.

The boy was ready, bubbling with excitement, and skipping about in a way that rather vexed the President of the Literary Society. They took a turn down Buckingham Park Road, and then—having seen that no one was watching them—slipped up the alley. Naturally enough (for the sun was setting) they ran straight against the omnibus.

"Good heavens!" exclaimed Mr. Bons. "Good gracious heavens!"

It was not the omnibus in which the boy had driven first, nor yet that in which he had returned. There were three horses—black, gray, and white, the gray being the finest. The driver, who turned round at the mention of goodness and of heaven, was a sallow man with terrifying jaws and sunken eyes. Mr. Bons, on seeing him, gave a cry as if of recognition, and began to tremble violently.

The boy jumped in.

"Is it possible?" cried Mr. Bons. "Is the impossible possible?"

"Sir; come in, sir. It is such a fine omnibus. Oh, here is his name—Dan some one."

Mr. Bons sprang in too. A blast of wind immediately slammed the omnibus door, and the shock jerked down all the omnibus blinds, which were very weak on their springs.

"Dan . . . Show me. Good gracious heavens! we're moving."

"Hooray!" said the boy.

Mr. Bons became flustered. He had not intended to be kidnapped. He could not find the doorhandle, nor push up the blinds. The omnibus was quite dark, and by the time he had struck a match, night had come on outside also. They were moving rapidly.

"A strange, a memorable adventure," he said, surveying the interior of the omnibus, which was large, roomy, and constructed with extreme regularity, every part exactly answering to every other part. Over the door (the handle of which was outside) was written, "Lasciate ogni baldanza voi che entrate" at least, that was what was written, but Mr. Bons said that it was Lashy arty something, and that baldanza was a mistake for speranza. His voice sounded as if he was in church. Meanwhile, the boy called to the cadaverous driver for two return tickets. They were handed in without a word. Mr. Bons covered his face with his hands and again trembled. "Do you know who that is!" he whispered, when the little window had shut upon them. "It is the impossible."

"Well, I don't like him as much as Sir Thomas Browne, though I shouldn't be surprised if he had even more in him."

"More in him?" He stamped irritably. "By accident you have made the greatest discovery of the century, and all you can say is that there is more in this man. Do you remember those vellum books in my library, stamped with red lilies? This—sit still, I bring you stupendous news!—*this is the man who wrote them.*"

The boy sat quite still. "I wonder if we shall see Mrs. Gamp?" he asked, after a civil pause.

"Mrs.—?"

"Mrs. Gamp and Mrs. Harris. I like Mrs. Harris. I came upon them quite suddenly. Mrs. Gamp's bandboxes have moved over the rainbow so badly. All the bottoms have fallen out, and two of the pippins off her bedstead tumbled into the stream."

"Out there sits the man who wrote my vellum books!" thundered Mr. Bons, "and you talk to me of Dickens and of Mrs. Gamp?"

"I know Mrs. Gamp so well," he apologized. "I could not help being glad to see her. I recognized her voice. She was telling Mrs. Harris about Mrs. Prig."

"Did you spend the whole day in her elevating company?"

"Oh, no. I raced. I met a man who took me out beyond to a race course. You run, and there are dolphins out at sea."

"Indeed. Do you remember the man's name?"

"Achilles. No; he was later. Tom Jones."

Mr. Bons sighed heavily. "Well, my lad, you have made a miserable mess of it. Think of a cultured person with your opportunities! A cultured person would have known all these characters and known what to have said to each. He would not have wasted his time with a Mrs. Gamp or a Tom Jones. The creations of Homer, of Shakespeare, and of Him who drives us now, would alone have contented him. He would not have raced. He would have asked intelligent questions."

"But, Mr. Bons," said the boy humbly, "you will be a cultured person. I told them so."

"True, true, and I beg you not to disgrace me when we arrive. No gossiping. No running. Keep close to my side, and never speak to these Immortals unless they speak to you. Yes, and give me the return tickets. You will be losing them."

The boy surrendered the tickets, but felt a little sore.

After all, he had found the way to this place. It was hard first to be disbelieved and then to be lectured. Meanwhile, the rain had stopped, and moonlight crept into the omnibus through the cracks in the blinds.

"But how is there to be a rainbow?" cried the boy.

"You distract me," snapped Mr. Bons. "I wish to meditate on beauty. I wish to goodness I was with a reverent and sympathetic person."

The lad bit his lip. He made a hundred good resolutions. He would imitate Mr. Bons all the visit. He would not laugh, or run, or sing, or do any of the vulgar things that must have disgusted his new friends last time. He would be very careful to pronounce their names properly, and to remember who knew whom. Achilles did not know Tom Jones—at least, so Mr. Bons said. The Duchess of Malfi was older than Mrs. Gamp—at least, so Mr. Bons said. He would be self-conscious, reticent, and prim. He would never say he liked any one. Yet, when the blind flew up at a chance touch of his head, all these good resolutions went to the winds, for the omnibus had reached the summit of a moonlit hill, and there was the chasm, and there, across it, stood the old precipices, dreaming, with their feet in the everlasting river. He exclaimed, "The mountain! Listen to the new tune in the water! Look at the camp fires in the ravines," and Mr. Bons, after a hasty glance, retorted, "Water? Camp fires? Ridiculous rubbish. Hold your tongue. There is nothing at all."

Yet, under his eyes, a rainbow formed, compounded not of sunlight and storm, but of moonlight and the spray of the river. The three horses put their feet upon it. He thought it the finest rainbow he had seen, but did not dare to say so, since Mr. Bons said that nothing was there. He leant out —the window had opened—and sang the tune that rose from the sleeping waters.

"The prelude to Rhinegold?" said Mr. Bons suddenly. "Who taught you these *leit motifs?*" He, too, looked out of the window. Then he behaved very oddly. He gave a choking cry, and fell back on to the omnibus floor. He writhed and kicked. His face was green.

"Does the bridge make you dizzy?" the boy asked.

"Dizzy!" gasped Mr. Bons. "I want to go back. Tell the driver."

But the driver shook his head.

"We are nearly there," said the boy. "They are asleep. Shall I call? They will be so pleased to see you, for I have prepared them."

Mr. Bons moaned. They moved over the lunar rainbow, which ever and ever broke away behind their wheels. How still the night was! Who would be sentry at the Gate?

"I am coming," he shouted, again forgetting the hundred resolutions. "I am returning—I, the boy."

"The boy is returning," cried a voice to other voices, who repeated, "The boy is returning."

"I am bringing Mr. Bons with me."

Silence.

"I should have said Mr. Bons is bringing me with him."

Profound silence.

"Who stands sentry?"

"Achilles."

And on the rocky causeway, close to the springing of the rainbow bridge, he saw a young man who carried a wonderful shield.

"Mr. Bons, it is Achilles, armed."

"I want to go back," said Mr. Bons.

The last fragment of the rainbow melted, the wheels sang upon the living rock, the door of the omnibus burst open. Out leapt the boy—he could not resist—and sprang to meet the warrior, who, stooping suddenly, caught him on his shield.

"Achilles!" he cried, "let me get down, for I am ignorant and vulgar, and I must wait for that Mr. Bons of whom I told you yesterday."

But Achilles raised him aloft. He crouched on the wonderful shield, on heroes and burning cities, on vineyards graven in gold, on every dear passion, every joy, on the entire image of the Mountain that he had discovered, encircled, like it, with an everlasting stream. "No, no," he protested, "I am not worthy. It is Mr. Bons who must be up here."

But Mr. Bons was whimpering, and Achilles trumpeted and cried, "Stand upright upon my shield!"

"Sir, I did not mean to stand! something made me stand. Sir, why do you delay? Here is only the great Achilles, whom you knew."

Mr. Bons screamed, "I see no one. I see nothing. I want to go back." Then he cried to the driver, "Save me! Let me stop in your chariot. I have honoured you. I have quoted you. I have bound you in vellum. Take me back to my world."

The driver replied, "I am the means and not the end. I am the food and not the life. Stand by yourself, as that boy has stood. I cannot save you. For poetry is a spirit; and they that would worship it must worship in spirit and in truth."

Mr. Bons—he could not resist—crawled out of the beautiful omnibus. His face appeared, gaping horribly. His hands followed, one gripping the step, the other beating the air. Now his shoulders emerged, his chest, his stomach. With a shriek of "I see London," he fell—fell against the hard, moonlit rock, fell into it as if it were water, fell through it, vanished, and was seen by the boy no more.

"Where have you fallen to, Mr. Bons? Here is a procession arriving to honour you with music and torches. Here come the men and women whose names you know. The mountain is awake, the river is awake, over the race-course the sea is awaking those dolphins, and it is all for you. They want you—"

There was the touch of fresh leaves on his forehead. Some one had crowned him.

ΤΕΔΟΣ

From the *Kingston Gazette, Surbiton Times,*
and *Raynes Park Observer.*

The body of Mr. Septimus Bons has been found in a shockingly mutilated condition in the vicinity of the Bermondsey gas-works. The deceased's pockets contained a sovereign-purse, a silver cigar-case, a bijou pronouncing dictionary, and a couple of omnibus tickets. The unfortunate gentleman had apparently been hurled from a considerable height. Foul play is suspected, and a thorough investigation is pending by the authorities.

Sophy

SUBSCRIPTION INFORMATION

Sophy, the Journal of Inspired Writing, is issued four times a year. Individual copies cost $9.99 and can be purchased at any bookstore or from the publisher. Subscriptions to an entire year of the journal can be purchased for $32, a savings of $8 off the newstand price. Subscriptions for two years cost only $55; for three years, $72.

To subscribe, send a check or money order (no cash) to Kudzu House, P.O. Box 297, Marble Hill, GA 30148. Or call toll free 1 (800) 336-7769 Mondays through Thursdays from 10 to 5 and charge the order to MasterCard, VISA, Diners, American Express, or Discover. Our e-mail address is light@stc.net.

Back issues may be ordered from Kudzu House.